Isidor Bush

Our Widows and Orphans Endowments

A study - Dedicated to the members of the I.O.B.B.

Isidor Bush

Our Widows and Orphans Endowments
A study - Dedicated to the members of the I.O.B.B.

ISBN/EAN: 9783337387839

Printed in Europe, USA, Canada, Australia, Japan

Cover: Foto ©Andreas Hilbeck / pixelio.de

More available books at **www.hansebooks.com**

OUR
Widows and Orphans
Endowments.

A STUDY.

DEDICATED TO THE MEMBERS OF T HE

I. O. B. B.

BY THEIR BROTHER

ISIDOR BUSH.

NEW YORK:
PHIL. COWEN, PRINTER,
Office of THE AMERICAN HEBREW 498-500 Third Avenue.
-1895.

OUR WIDOW AND ORPHAN ENDOWMENTS.

Part I.—A Study of Its Early History.

To provide for the widow and orphan is one
of the principal tenets of our Order. From the
first constitution of New York Lodge, No. 1, established in 1843, to the latest version of our
Organic Law, now in force, the duty of "pro
viding for, protecting and assisting the widow and
orphan on the broadest principles of humanity,"
was ever inculated, and has been faithfully observed by its members.[1]

At first, each lodge had its own small Widow
and Orphan fund, from which a quarterly stipend
was to be paid; but this proved insufficient, unsatisfactory, and at the same time burdensome,
aye, ruinous to our old lodges.[2]

[1]. The Preamble to that first Constitution contained the
words ; " die Wittwen und Waisen ihrer verstorbenen
Brüder zu unterstuetzen und denselben nach Kraften ihren
Rath und Schutz angedeihen zu lassen."

[2]. Proceedings of D. G. L. No. 1, 1866-1867, pages

If our younger members, and our older ones
who have forgotten many things—if they, who
"yearn for the days of yore, when our Order
was sought for its noble aims and objects only,"
—"when the beneficence to the needy widow
and orphan directly bestowed by the Lodge,
by means of her widow and orphan fund, or
otherwise was far in excess to the advantages

138–144, contain a very able and interesting Committee's
report, from which we extract the following:

" This brings us to contemplate the present mode of
supporting the widows and orphans of deceased brethren.
In the best days of any lodge, the highest rate of annual
benefit to a widow is $50, and to an orphan it is $25 per
annum. This benefit is so small that at the present prices
of rent, provisions and clothing, it is even too little to
starve the widow and her children. Yet even this small
pittance is not in the power of many of the Sections to give
at all times, and some of our oldest Sections have been
compelled, by reason of increased mortality amongst their
members, to reduce the rate of these benefits. What has
happened in one Section is precisely what inevitably must
happen in all the other Sections laboring under the same
conditions. Increased mortality will in rotation fall upon
all the Sections..... The truth is, our widows' and orphans'
funds have too small income for the extensive but insufficient benefits they give "

The report then goes on to show by some very plain
figuring that: "*It is, then, mathematically certain that in this
matter of Benefit all Sections will finally fail, and the
sacred promises made to Brothers will have to remain unful-
filled by the force of circumstances.*"

derived from the $1,ooo Endowment benefit"—if
our brethren, who thus speak and believe, would
refer to the printed proceedings of our various
Grand Lodges in those halcyon days,—they
would find that then also the question of *benefit*
to our widows and orphans was a matter of interest, of anxiety and of dissatisfaction.[3]

In October, 1868, after long debates on various
plans proposed by its several committees, D. G.
L. No. 1 agreed on a substitute offered by Bro.
Julius Bien, amending the constitution, and re-

---

3. On January 30th, 1868, D. G. L. No. 1 adopted the
following resolutions :

WHEREAS, It is one of the chief aims of the Order and
principal duties incumbent on its members to provide for
the widows and orphans; and

WHEREAS. The condition of the younger lodges, or more
properly of their Widows' and Orphans' fund, is such as to
incapacitate them from extending any aid : and

WHEREAS, The call upon the old lodges is in many cases
at present so extensive (and may even become more so) as
not to allow them to fulfill these obligations towards the
families of each of them as are and may become deceased;
therefore

Resolved, 1. That an Association be established under
the supervision of the M. W. G. Officers of the District,
to be known as the B. B. Relief Association. 2. That all
brothers shall be entitled to membership in this Association
by paying $2 initiation fee and $1 each on the death of any
member of the Association, etc. 3. That a Committee be
appointed to draw proper laws and rules for regulating and
furthering the objects of said Association.

quiring every brother of the Order in this District to pay the sum of 25 cts. at the death of a member in good standing—to be paid over to the widow or designated representatives of the deceased brother.[4]   This was *the first District Endowment Law*; it was finally adopted at the general annual session of D. G. L. No. 1, Jan. 24th, 1869, with only two dissenting votes.[4]

---

4. Bro. Julius Bien offered as a substitute the following (the proceedings were then held in German.):

" Die Mangelhaftigkeit des gegenwärtigen Unterstützungsplanes für Hinterlassene verstorbener Brüder der Logen dieses Districts neben der Unzulänglichkeit der ge botenen Hilfe, hat seit geraumer Zeit die Aufmerksamkeit denkender Brüder in Anspruch genommen und sind in Folge dessen verschiedene Entwürfe zur kraeftigern und sicheren Unterstützung der Witwen and Waisen dieser Grossloge unterbreitet und von derselben in Berathung gezogen worden. In der letzt abgehaltenen Special Versammlung hat die Grossloge, als die geeigneteste Erledigung dieser wichtigen Frage beschlossen, § 5. Art. 1. dritte Autheilung der Gesetze dieses Districts auf folgender Weise zu amendiren."

Nach den Worten, "den Betrag der regelmässigen Beiträge festsetzen," werde hinzugefügt : " Doch soll jeder Bruder des Ordens in diesem Districte beim Ableben eines vollberechtigten Mitgliedes einer Loge dieses Districts, die Summe von 25 cents bezahlen."

" Der Secretär der Loge, in der ein vollberechtigtes Mitglied gestorben, soll sogleich alle Logen dieses Districts von dem Sterbfalle in Kenntniss setzen und jede Loge dieses Districts soll die Summe von 25 cents für jedes ihrer Mitglieder an die betreffende Loge innerhalb 30 Tage aus zahlen und solche 25 cents als regelmässigen Beitrag von

Warning voices, however, were not altogether missing. On' that day already, many representatives expressed the fear that in time the mortality would become much larger; and they tried to prove this by figures and arguments; but Bro. Friedlein's statistical table, showing that from

---

jedem ihrer Mitglieder bei nächster Einzahlung erheben Die Gesammtsumme aller solchen Beiträge soll von den Trustees der betreffenden Loge der Wittwe oder den gesetzlichen Erben (amended : or designated representatives) des verstorbenen Bruders sofort ausgezahlt werden."

Die Schlussgiltige Abstimmung über diesen Vorschlag findet in der General Versammlung der Grossloge im naechsten Monate statt und ist derselbe ihrer ernsten und reiflichen Ueberlegung empfohlen, damit ihre Representanten zur Zeit in ihrem und ihres Districts bestem Interesse ihr Votum abgeben.

Ihrer Aufmerksamkeit kann die einfache Weise, in der hier ein grosser Zweck erreicht wird nicht entgehen......
Bei der jetzigen Mitgliederzahl des Districtes würde unter solchen Umständen eine Wittwe ungefähr neun hundert dollars erhalten, eine Summe, die in den meisten Verhältnissen ausreichend sein dürfte, ihr genügende Mittel zur Erwerbung eines Lebensunterhaltes in die Hände zu geben. Sollte, wie voraussichtlich, die Anzahl der Mitglieder sich so vermehren, dass der erzielte Betrag die Summe von Tausend Dollars ubersteigt, so könnte der Beitrag entsprechend verringert-werden.

Es ist selbstverständlich dass dann auch fernere Beitrage für einen Wittwen und Waisen-fond nicht erforderlich sind, und sie werden bei genauer Prüfung finden das durch die Annahme dieses Planes den Brüdern keine grossen Lasten auferlegt werden, vielmehr mit denselben Mitteln,—die unter dem alten System, manche Logen bis *an den Rand*

1851–1868 the number of our deaths never reached even one per cent, seemed to refute them
completely. They overlooked the fact that for
every member who died more than ten new
younger members joined at that time; or, if they
noticed it, did not understand that such an increase of membership *retards* the advance in
average age; they were even led to believe that
the advance in age, and consequent increase in
mortality, could be forever prevented by the addition of new members!

In vain did Ararat Lodge, No. 13, in an earnest and able appeal protest against the new law;
in vain, soon thereafter, did two lodges appeal
against District Grand Lodge No. 3, and one
against District Grand Lodge No. 4, which adopted similar endowment laws.

-----

des finanziellen Ruins gebracht und alle gefæhrdet haben,
ohne wesentliche Unterstutzung zu bieten —einer der edels-
ten Zwecke des Ordens Sorge zu tragen für die Hinterblie-
benen verstorbener Brüder, auf sichere und nachhaltige
Weise erzielt wird."

In December, 1868, a circular was addressed to all the
lodges in District No. 1, calling their attention to the imperfect system then in existence of aiding the families of
deceased brethren, its total insufficiency to supply the
needs of widows and orphans, its dangers to the financial
position of the lodges, and also to the proposed amendment
of the laws as a remedy.

The Court of Appeals decided their enactment to be constitutional and valid.[5] In vain did a few brethren, better informed on the subject, endeavor to show the defects and instability of the system,—the demand for its adoption became irrepressibe in all our districts. The failure of the lodge's widow and orphan fund, the insufficiency of the support thereby given to the families of deceased brethren (out of every five deaths there were always two, sometimes three, cases in which the sister lodges had to be appealed to for assistance), and the great popularity and seeming success obtained by many new so-called Co-operative or Assesment Insurance Associations, just then formed all over the country and adopted by some fraternal societies—all these circumstances combined—have led to the early adoption of endowment fund laws in almost every District of our Order. The only exception was District No. 2, where a voluntary B. B. Endowment Association had been organized as early as Nov. 1867. And in this case also the lodges outside of Cincinnati, especially those in the South, insisted on the adoption of a District

5. Appeals III. and IV. Report 1868-1870. Pages 7-8, and Appeal xiii., Report 1873, p. 132.

Endowment Law;[6] so much so, that the G. N. A.'s (President's) Message to the Grand Lodge at the opening of its session, on Jan. 21st, 1882, contained the following words: "In many, and especially in our Southern lodges, the desire for

6. At the 18th annual meeting of D. G. L. No. 2, held at Nashville, Tenn., in Jan., 1870, Emanuel Lodge, No. 103, of Montgomery, Ala., presented a petition to establish an Endowment Association, "similar to those established in Districts 1, 3 and 6," wherein it is stated that "Many of the lodges in this District have been consulted. From a large majority of them favorable answers have been received." It was referred to a special committee of five, and they reported unanimously in favor " That a general Endowment Fund be established in this District No. 2." But it did not receive the required two-third vote. In 1871, the Missouri lodges presented a memorial, ''asking the District Grand Lodge to pass some law for a General Endowment fund throughout the District.'' The majority report in favor of it was adopted, aud the minority report even said : "Seeing as I do the very successful operation of an Endowment Association in Cincinnati, I strongly favor the establishment of similar societies wherever they can be successfully and practically carried out " the only objections being that it did not approve of a forcible (compulsory) assessment, and that it would be "too unwieldy ' over so large a territory. But the proposition failed to receive the vote of the majority of the Lodges, and was therefore declared rejected.

the organization of an Endowment fund is so strong that *it may become the cause and the principal motive for a separation from District No. 2.*[7] On the other hand, the opposition to its establishment in the lodges of Ohio was mainly due to the apprehension that it might interfere with the progress of the endowment association already existing and in *supposed* prosperous operation, at Cincinnati. Another organization of this kind, also organized by and for members of our Order, at Memphis, Tenn., being aware of the difficulties arising from a too limited membership, desired to enlarge its field of operation within the fraternity; while again some lodges favor, and some have lately established, local and even separate endowment funds, compelling its members to pay as high as five dollars on the death

---

7. The Southern lodges did separate, forming our District No. 7. The official report on the installation of this new Grand Lodge (on January 19th, 1873,) says : " Probably this determination (to oppose the introduction of an Endowment Law, general in its application,) on the part ot Lodges of Dist. No. 2, situated in a more Northern climate, hastened the establishment of an independent Southern Grand Lodge, as the members residing in the South were determined, and justly so, not to be deprived of the benefits of this wise law."

of a brother."[8] In this Message, the President of the District warned the brethren against errors, "errors already committed, which must prove detrimental to the future welfare of the Order." He admits that: "To secure at the death of every member to his widow, orphans or heirs, an amount equal to the aggregate stipulated contributions of the remaining members, seems so simple, plain and cheap an insurance, that it appears to have advantages which naturally recommend it to a favorable consideration, so much so that not only in our own, but in nearly every fraternity similar benevolent, so-called co-operative insurance associations exist, or have been formed from time to time.

But have they been successful ? "

He answered this question by telling them that "their history is one of failures," that "all failed or had to be abandoned until they adopted fixed rates and other regulations based upon sound principles and correct calculation. It is true that many similar endowment associations do *now* exist, and seem to do well; but how long does any one of these exist ?....The friends of these institutions are charmed with the *present* good

8. Solomon Lodge, No. 16, at Cleveland, O.

results and care little for the future?....They
calculate thus: For every member lost by death
at least one other member, and likely a younger
one, is added, and the rate of mortality will remain the same. This rate, they believe (and
bring in as evidence the last 20 years' record of
our Order) will never exceed *one* per cent.—This
calculation is utterly erroneous."

The message then tries, by arguments and figures to convince the members of the fallacy of
such assumptions. In view of the fact, however,
that the demand for an Endowment fund was
irrepressible, the President tries in that message
to *"open the way for a correct future solution of
this problem."*

But his warning voice could not prevent the
passage of an Endowment Law at that session.
Propositions for an Endowment Law of the District were presented,9 and after several days' de-
liberation *one* was adopted;10 this being submitted

---

9. One emanating from the Memphis Lodges, in which
every member was to be a contributing and participating
member, and one from Cincinnati, in which membership
was to be voluntary.

10. This was the first and only endowment plan in our
Order which proposed graded assessments according to the

to the lodges of the District, 28 voted in favor and only 11 against it.

An appeal against this law was at once taken to the Court of Appeals, and it was decided "*Unconstitutional for its non-uniformity.*

But this by no means ended or quieted the agitation.[11]

---

age of the members. The constitution of District No. 2, however, provided that the D. G. L. shall have power to pass a law to create a General fund of the District, by levying a *uniform* contribution on all the members of the several lodges in the District.

11. At the January meeting, 1873, the report of the Committee to whom the Message of the G. N. A. was referred contained the following :

"We beg to call the attention of the worthy D. G. L. to the almost universal desire to lay before them some practical plan of Endowment at this session. Whilst the project of the Endowment as passed last year, both in convention and by the sub-lodges, has only been defeated by technical defects of the law, we feel that it is not only the urgent desire of the majority of the lodges, but also of the members thereof, to again prepare such a bill or a plan for adoption, but we also feel that the very existence of our beloved District is endangered if we pass this important question in silence "

A committee was appointed, but was unable to agree, and a recommendation or suggestion, that "it is the universal desire of the Order at large to establish a General Endowment of the whole Order, when in session in Chicago in 1874, which not alone would be cheap as to its support, but

In January, 1874, the Message of the then
G. N. A. of District No. 2, contains the following:

"Shortly after the adjournment of the last annual
meeting of the D. G. L., there was great dissension
and much disappointment and dissatisfaction expressed
by many lodges in our District, for the non-enactment
of an Endowment Law. In many lodges, the feelings
were so bitter, and the excitement grew so intense,
that a movement was set on foot to cut loose from
those sister lodges which so emphatically opposed, on
every occasion, each and every measure towards an
enactment of an Endowment law, and organize a new
Grand Lodge as District No. 8. It required all the
efforts of prominent and influential members in our
District to defeat this movement, and preserve harmony and unity. . . . It is far from my intention
to propose or recommend to you any plan for the
adoption of an Endowment Fund in this District at
this session, although out of s ven existing Districts
D. G. L. No. 2 is the *only one* where no general Endowment fund exists.

"Thus I take leave, therefore, to impress upon you
for favorable consideration the importance that D. G.
L. No. 2 should use all honorable means and efforts
in her power to secure a General Endowment Fund

also charitable and liberal in its bearings," was finally
adopted with 37 ayes against 14 nays.

throughout the whole Order, at the coming constitutional convention."

The thought that the District Endowment funds might be consolidated in the future was first expressed in the report of the Executive Committee for 1870.[12] It was again referred to in the report for 1872, and the confident belief expressed " that at the next regular convention of the Order this project will receive due attention, and in some form or other will be carried out by the framing of a general law."

The idea of *one general* Endowment-law seemed to meet with favor, not only in District No. 2, as already shown, but also in other Districts,[13] especially with members of broader views,

---

12. " A great improvement on the old, it is to be hoped that this new method will be generally introduced, and when thoroughly tested. its benefits enlarged and diffused by a consolidation of all the Districts. — *The President of the Exec. Com. Report*: *Jan.*, 1870. *p.* 17.

13. At the annual session of D. G. L. No. 6, held at Milwaukee, January, 1873, a committee report was adopted containing the following : " Upon this subject, the General Committee inform us that a digested scheme to make the Endowment Law a general one, embracing all districts in the Order, will likely be placed before the General Convention of 1874. The General Committee express no opinion on that subject. We cannot doubt for a moment that the broad principle of large heartedness and liberal judgment

whose great object was the strengthening of our union, the solidarity of the whole Order in measures for the general good—in contradiction to the separatism nurtured by a spirit of special interests and the creation of sectionalism—foremost among them its honored chief, whose clear, sound judgment, and whose pure devotion to our cause, are so well known. But in vain did he advocate this idea.[14] In vain did he accompany his report with a carefully prepared General Endowment plan, showing that an annual contribution of $15 from every member (then about 10,000 in number), or 10 cents at the death of a member, until the amount of $15 annually be reached, would produce a surplus during the *early* years which, invested at seven

---

which form the basis of action of this Grand Lodge will certainly prompt us to at once become the champions of the movement to secure a General Endowment Fund throughout the Order....... With all the brothers of the Order united in one grand Endowment Fund, even an epidemic that—God forbid—might visit any particular locality, would not be a severe strain upon the resources of the individual contributing member.......Besides, whenever we succeed in uniting all the brothers of the Order in the maintenance of any noble undertaking, we advance one step in the accomplishment of the very purpose of our existence."

14. Report of the Executive Committee, Jan., 1873.

per cent. interest, would form a reserve sufficient
to secure the permanency of the Endowment
institution. In vain did the terrible epidemic[15],
just then afflicting our Southern brethren, present
to thinking minds and warm hearts the great
advantages, if not the necessity, of *one general*
Widow and Orphan fund.

The Jewish press of this country was then
teeming with articles on the Endowment question. The plan for *one* general Endowment fund,
recommended in the Executive Committee report to the attention of the next General convention (meeting in Jan., 1874,) was antagonized
both by the opponents of all Endowment laws
and by the friends of their local or District Endowments lately organized. They denounced it
as a usurpation of power and as opposed to the
sovereignty of lodges ; as an unjust and even
unlawful scheme ; as oppressive to the poor ; as
a degradation of our Order to a mere Life-In
surance business ; as leading to fraud, even to
murder (!) ; as producing distrust, aye, rupture
between different sections of the country ; as

---

15. The yellow fever visited the cities of Shreveport and
Memphis with unparalelled virulence, and lasted for seven
weeks, from Sept. 9th to end of Oct., 1873.

creating a dangerous power and a monopoly ; as injurious to those fortunately situated Districts whom it behooves to *protect* themselves against those situated in sickly parts of the country ; as unnecessary, most of the Districts having their own separate Endowment laws, and as more expensive and unwieldy than these Districts Endowments.

These specious arguments and criticisms were, of course, also ably refuted in some of these journals ; but the seeds of discord were thrown in our midst, the clap-trap and sophistry deceived those at least who did not fully understand the proposed plan, or the fallacy of their local Endowment systems—and the result was, that very many lodges, those of District No. 1 almost in a body, instructed their delegates to the convention to vote against any and all propositions for *one* General Endowment fund of the Order.[16]

---

16. The General Committee of D. G. L. No. 1 had sub mitted to a convention of its lodges, held on June 29th, 1873, a series of " instructions to delegates to the Chicago convention," of which the 7th was as follows :

"7th. To instruct the representatives of District No. 1 to the Chicago convention to vote and work against the introduction of a general Endowment fund for the whole Or—

The convention met (in Chicago, Jan 25th–30th,
1874) ; a committee on Endowment, fairly composed of representatives of every District, with
the framer of the proposed General Endowment
plan as its chairman, was appointed. It was evident to all that neither the proposed nor any
other law contemplating a *General* Endowment
fund had any chance to obtain the required two-
third majority. The chairman, having no per-
sonal interest in the matter, and fully agreeing
with the President of the Order in the conviction
that, " *Whatever may be the fate of this proposition, general and uniform regulations of the Endowment plan are absolutely needed throughout the
districts of the Order,*"[17] he at once, in conjunction
with an eminent member of said committee

---

der, as it would be antagonistic to the interest of this District
and detrimental to the Order in general."

This was adopted, though the plan for a General Endowment fund, recommended in the Executive Committee's report, was not yet printed at that time, nor even known to
them. and, though about one–half of the members of that
convention had no credentials, the representatives of the
60 lodges of District No. 1, with very few exceptions, felt
themselves bound by those instructions.

17. Report of the Executive Committee of the C. G. L.,
Jan., 1872, to Jan., 1873. page 36

(from Dist. No. 1), prepared a District Endowment law, which left the direction, management and control to the District Grand Lodges, with only one feature of union or solidarity : that, in case of epidemics or other emergencies, a majority of the Executive Committee may order a levy of five cents on every member for each deceased brother, until such emergency shall have ceased.

But a majority of the committee would not agree to even this, and the chairman was in the unpleasant position not only of having to make a minority report, but one which he considered a mere compromise, of which he himself could not fully approve.

The majority of the committee simply declared " that in the present state of the Order it is inexpedient and premature to legislate by any general laws for an Endowment plan in our Order."

In the course of the discussion on these two reports, the chairman of the committee was asked whether he, as an expert, considered the plan reported by him as a sufficient safeguide to secure the stability of the Endowment, and he honestly replied that he did *not*, but that it seemed the best now attainable, and left to the District

Grand Lodges power to augment their reserve funds as experience might dictate. This, naturally, weakened the friends of the measure, so much so that even some of the most fervent advocates of the original general Endowment plan denounced the now proposed bill as "not what was wanted," and it was lost (54 voting in the affirmative, 78 in the negative). Several other propositions shared the same fate, until finally (on the fourth day of the convention) the following simple resolution was adopted:

Resolved, That the establishment of Widows' and Orphans' Endowment Funds, by District Grand Lodges, is within the legitimate scope of the aims and objects of the Order.

As soon as the proposition for a General Endowment Law was defeated, the representatives of the lodges of Michigan asked to be transferred to District No. 6, and a further division of District No. 2 was imminent, unless the lodges of Ohio and Indiana gave up their former opposition to the establishment of an Endowment fund. To prevent such an unfortunate occurrence, nearly all the delegates from District No. 2 assembled in caucus on that same night (Jan. 28th to 29th), and by a unanimous vote deter-

mined that, within sixty days, a special meeting
of this G. L. be convened at Cincinnati, in order
to enact a proper Endowment law for their District. And the delegates from Cincinnati pledged
themselves to use proper efforts with their lodges
to elect representatives favoring the measure.

Within two months from the adjournment of
the convention District Grand Lodge No. 2
held the special meeting, (on March 1, 1874),
and an Endowment law, framed on the same plan
as the one originally recommended by the Executive Committee for the whole Order, was
adopted by a *unanimous* vote.[18]

Every District had now its Endowment Law.
All were pleased with the practical, beneficent
working of the system ; it seemed to work so
well ! Over one hundred thousand dollars were
paid annually to our members' widows and or-

---

18. Twenty-four lodges were fully represented, four only
unrepresented, 53 representatives voting aye, *none* in the
negative ; and, though the old persistent opposition set to
work to make the lodges refuse their assent, over two—
thirds of the lodges had ratified the law as soon as submitted. On May 1st, 1874, it went into operation. and 26
lodges remitted the initiation fee for their members.

phans, without anyone feeling it a burden ; the assessments were light. Why should it not ever so remain ?

Our Endowment system differs from that of
most other associations formed for the purpose
of securing the benefits of life insurance by assessments. These Mutual Benefit Associations con-
sist either of members organized for this purpose, without other ties or obligations, and se-
lected under certain restrictions as to age and
condition of health, or of members of fraternal
organizations, of which, however, those only are
admitted to such insurance schemes who can
comply with similar conditions and are willing to
pay assessments graded according to age.[1]

---

[1]   The ninth annual convention of Mutual Benefit Assessment Associations adopted the following : ''No Organization shall be eligible to membership...that shall not have its
rates of assessment graded according to one, or, the combined standard mortality tables; or, when a uniform rate is
charged, that shall not have its *benefits* graded according to
the tables of life expectation, or that does not use proper
precaution in selection; or, that does not protect the en-
trants, or new member, at any time in its history—*by increasing the rate with advancing age of the insured, or by*

Our fraternity, the I. O. B. B., existed over a quarter of a century before the Endowment feature was introduced. It was not conceived as an insurance scheme, but simply as a better method of supporting the widows and orphans of our brethren. Our Endowment plans are broader and more liberal, embracing *all* our members at a uniform rate. They are irresistibly demanded by our lodges (as shown in Part I, "its early history") are demanded as a necessity, as a duty we owe to each other, and especially to the older brethren, to those who had worked earnestly and zealously for the great, noble objects of our Order, and who might soon depart from us—relying on the aid and assistance of the younger element for their widows and orphans.

Ours is a charity—theirs is a business.

Charity does not carefully weigh her gifts nor coldly figure her resources ; she gives.

"Pity dwelleth in her bosom,
Kindness reigneth o'er her heart,
Gentle thoughts alone can stir her,
Judgment hath in her no part."

Hence the framers of our Endowment-institu-

accumulating a fund in lieu of increasing rates,—against being assessed more than the natural premium, as indicated

tion, in its early inception, may well be pardoned for not having studied the questions of vital statistics, or "what will be the rate of mortality in future years?" nor having calculated anything, except : "How much should each member give at the demise of a brother to enable us to give about $1,000 to his bereaved family?[2]

---

by the Am. Mortality Experience Table; ......*Provided*, this article shall not be applicable to Fraternal Societies *already organized*, where there are ties other than mere business considerations."

2. Our first Widow and Orphan Endowment Law, adopted by D. G. L. No. 1, Jan. 23, 1869, provided: That at the death of a brother in good standing, every brother of the Order in this District shall pay the sum of twenty-five cents ; (the District then had about 4,000 members) ; that every Lodge of the District shall forward twenty-five cents for every one of its members to the Lodge wherein the death occurred, and that the total amount so collected shall be handed over at once. by the Trustee of the respective Lodge, to the widow, or legal heirs, or designated repre sentatives of the deceased brother.

The General Committee was requested to report to the next meeting of the Grand Lodge a more detailed and perfected Endowment Law, *with a view to secure perfect equality and safety in its operation.*

In January 1871 said committee did report a new Endowment law which limited the amount of the endowments to *one thousand dollars* in each case, leaving it to the Grand

This seemed so simple and safe, so easily carried out, yet so perfectly securing the desired object—a more effective aid to the widows and

Lodge to determine, from year to year, the amount of assessment, so as to be sufficient to secure at least one thousand dollars by equal contributions from all its members. And the surplus over $1,000, resulting from such assessment, was to be transmitted to the Grand Lodge, which would make proper disposition of the same. (Proceedings D. G. L. No. 1, Jan. 1871, pp. 46 and 47.)

The Grand Lodge actually resolved that "as soon as this surplus will amount to $2,000, the Endowments for the next two cases of death shall be paid therefrom without making for same any assessment on the Lodges," and on February 5, 1872, such disposition of the first two thousand dollars of (supposed) surplus was actually made.

On Jan. 27, 1873, this Grand Lodge again resolved that the surplus of $9,000, then accumulated in their W. and O Endowment Fund be used in paying the next nine death-claims, and the per capita tax towards that fund was reduced to seventeen cents. Every proposition to keep this surplus as a reserve fund, or at least not to reduce the tax below twenty cents, was voted down.

District No. 3 provided in its Endowment Law for assessments of fifty cents for each member, and that the total amount received be handed over by the Trustee of the respective Lodge to the widow, if there be any; or, if there be no widow, to the children or their legal guardians, etc. This was afterwards so amended that "each Lodge of this

orphans of deceased brethren, without any of the former frequent appeals for their support—that scarcely anything further seemed necessary.

A Reserve-fund, to provide against *possible*

District shall be so assessed as to make the sum of one thousand dollars. The assessment shall be made by the Secretary of the Grand Lodge, pro rata, according to the number of members reported by each lodge for the preceding quarter, and any fractional surplus received shall be set aside, and when it shall amount to a sufficient sum, it shall be appropriated to the payment of the next death occurring."

In District No. 6, an Endowment Fund had been in operation since September 1869. In accordance with its provisions one dollar per capita was collected at the death of a brother, and the full amount paid over to the widow, or, in absence thereof, to the legal representatives of the deceased brother. This D. G. L. was the first to place the management of its Endowment fund in the hands of a board of trustees, and to contemplate something like a sinking fund, which was to be derived, however, "from voluntary contributions, donations and legacies of individuals and brothers, as well as of the several lodges, or from any other source."

In District No. 4 an Endowment fund went into effect from the 23d of February, 1872—each lodge being required to pay $1.25 for every member, at the death of a brother, and the whole amount so collected was to be paid to the widow, etc.

contingencies, and for the *certain* increase of mortality in later years, was so little thought of that in all of our first District-Endowment laws the entire amount resulting from an assessment was given to the family of the deceased brother Soon afterwards the Endowment was limited to \$1000, *but then also*, the excess above that amount, received by such assessments, was to be used for paying endowments as soon as it would be sufficient for such purpose.[3]

The only difficulties that seemed to present themselves in the beginning, were:

1. The irregularities and delays in transmitting the Endowment dues and consequently in the payments to the beneficiaries, etc.[4]

---

3. In District No. 7, however, the sum of fifteen hundred dollars was to be secured to the widow of a deceased member by assessments of one dollar for every member of the District. "And whenever the surplus thus received above said amount shall reach the amount of \$1500 or more, the sum shall be employed in paying the next endowment, and when so adjusted, the assessment provided for in Sect. 4, shall not be levied."

4. From the report of a committee appointed by D. G. L., No. 1, to revise the W. and O. Endowment Law, dated June 5, 1872, we quote: Durch das öftere Wechseln der Beamten, und mitunter durch Unfähigkeit derselben, ent-

2. The extensive and frequently useless correspondence, in matters of the Endowment-law, between the various Lodges and their respective District Grand Lodge, increasing the labor and absorbing the attention of the General Committees to the detriment of their other affairs.5

3. The complications and questions as to the rights of beneficiaries, arising from the terms "legal heirs" and "legal representatives" of de-

----

steht in vielen Fällen solche Verzögerung, dass die Hinterlassenen eines verstorbenen Bruders zuweilen ihre Bezüge eist nach Ablauf von drei oder vier Monaten erhalten und die Ueberschüsse mitunter erst nach Ablauf eines Jahres und meistens sehr unvollkommen in die Hände der Gross-Loge gelangen. In January 1874 the Grand Sopher of District No. 1 had still to call the attention of the Grand Lodge to the negligence of some lodges in failing to send their proper proportion of the amounts due for endowment in proper time, notwithstanding the frequent notices sent to them."

5. The heretofore quoted Report of the General Committee of D. G. L. No 1. contains the following:

1) Erzeugt die Ausführung desselben (des W. u. W. Unterstützungs Gesetzes) eine umfangreiche und mitunter nicht sehr erspriessliche Correspondenz, sowohl für die Distr. Gross-Loge, als auch für die Logen selbst...........
und ist zu erwarten, dass die anderweitigen Geschäfte der Gross-Loge durch diese besondere Auflage merklich beeinträchtigt werden.

ceased brethren, which terms are still used in most of our District Endowment laws.[6]

---

6.   As early as 1871 the question arose, in the case of Bro Reblaub, of Hillel Lodge No. 28, as to how to act, the deceased brother having no heirs in this country, but in Europe and in South America. The cases of Bro. Phil. L. Bachman of N. Y. Lodge No. 1, and of Bro. Emil Indig, of Manhattan Lodge No. 156, which gave rise to considerable disputes and appeals (See Proceedings of D. G. L. No. 1 of 1874-75, pp. 57-66 : also pp. 89-96; also pp. 103, 106-109, and Court of Appeals, Appeal No. 21; Report 1874-1875, pp. 76 132.) involved the question of the claim of alleged *heirs* to the Endowment.

I. A. STODDARD, Sec'y N. W. Masonic Aid Association, in an essay on "The Law governing Beneficiaries, says :

"There are several very nice and intricate questions involved in the use of this term *"legal heirs,"* which render this manner of writing certificates very undesirable and one which we should seek to avoid as much as possible.   This term *"legal heirs"* is very indefinite.   It is a term used to designate certain persons unknown to us......it may mean one person to day and another to-morrow, and so on ; and many law-suits have already been tried to determine who were meant in certain cases, where the term has been used ......and to our own difficulties may be added contention among the heirs themselves."

A Committee, appointed by the Convention of Mutual Benefit Associations reported on this subject a recommendation—

"That all Associations be particular in requiring all applicants for membership to state distinctly and definitely the names of the beneficiaries, and, in case of the death of

These difficulties were soon overcome by changes in the management, in the mode of collection, etc., special standing committees, or

———

~~gave the following written opinion: "The plan or law of~~ the beneficiary before the death of the member, the application should also clearly designate the person or persons to succeed to the benefit."

M. ULMAN, G. S. of D. G. L. No. 7, in his great work "Jurisprudence of the I. O. B. B.," page 754 says: "To designate '*legal heirs,*' (as beneficiaries of an Endowment) opens the way for litigation, and the benefit intended to be an act of benevolence and an assistance to beneficiaries, becomes a bone of contention, a benefit to lawyers, and a prey to courts. To designate *legal heirs* is not a legal designation. It is not sufficient, under the provision of the Endowment-law, for a brother who, in case of death, would leave neither widow nor orphans, to designate that his legal heirs should receive the endowment......To prevent litigation, every brother should designate by name the party or parties he intends to benefit by his endowment."

District Grand Lodge No. 4 *decided* that it is not suffi cient, under the provisions of the Endowment-law, for a brother who, in case of death, would leave neither widow nor orphans, to designate that his legal heirs should receive the endowment. (Proceedings 1873, pp. 46, 47.)

In this connection it is proper to remark that the provisions contained in most of our District Endowment-laws, giving widowers or unmarried members the right to designate any person or persons, other than members of his family or charitable institutions, as beneficiaries, is not only contrary to the spirit and object of our Endowment institutions, but

Boards of Trustees being appointed for these purposes.[7]

The members were proud of the many praises

contrary to the laws of most of our States. Hon. Judge
GEO. HOADLEY, one of the first jurists of this country, now
Governor of Ohio, to whom the question was submitted,
gave the following written opinion: "The plan or law of
Endowment of District Grand Lodge No. 2 is lawful, ex-
'cept in one particular, viz., in permitting the benefits to
'accrue to 'designated beneficiaries.' This is Life Insur-
'ance, and not permissible under the incorporation of this
'body (for benevolent purposes). If the plan of Endow-
'ment should be amended so as to confine its operations to
'*members of the family and charitable institutions*, it will
'be unobjectionable." The Endowment-law of District
No. 2 was thereupon amended to that effect.

7. In January, 1873, the General Committee of District
Grand Lodge No. 1 recommended that the management of
its Endowment fund, its collections and payments be placed
in the hands of a standing committee (Fünfter Ausschuss.)
This recommendation being adopted in Jan. 1874, reduced
the number constituting such committee to three only. In
1877 the Grand Sopher of said District made the following
report to an Endowment Commission of District Grand
Lodge No. 6: "The change is so beneficial that a Lodge
need hardly ever to be reminded of paying her dues within
thirty days from receipt of the notice of death, and all death
claims are paid within thirty days from the date the Grand
Lodge is notified—while formerly, when the Lodges col-

bestowed upon our Order for having introduced this noble mode of immediately relieving the widow of a deceased brother. Every District was highly pleased with the working of its own Endowment-fund, and deemed it almost perfect. The favorable reports received from different Grand Lodges caused the Executive Committee to say in its report for 1874-1875 : " Widow and Orphan Endowment Institutions are now successfully established in every District of the Order. Disputes and differences are happily adjusted, and all opposition has been silenced by the practical, beneficial working of the system."

So firm was the belief in the safety of that system and its workings, that scarcely any attempts were made to provide for a proper Reserve fund. Although even as early as July, 1872, the General Committee of D. G. L. No. 1, in its report to the Grand Lodge, presented the question of securing the W. and O. Endowment institution, without overburdening the fraternity, at some future time, when the mortality should increase,[8] and

— . ---

lected and paid the Endowments, widows had sometimes to wait from four to six months."

8.   "Die Frage ist und muss sein .... hauptsächlich

although this subject was then referred to a committee, nothing was done. Every motion to let the small surplus from Endowment dues ac-cumulate, toward at least the beginning of a sinking fund was rejected, even the proposition of the Committee to postpone action with re-gard to the formation of a sinking fund until after the General Convention of the Order, to be held in January, 1874, it being assumed that laws would there be enacted with regard to the Endowment institution, placing it on an equal basis throughout the Order "9 — even this proposition was referred to the Lodges of the District that they might instruct their repre-sentatives as to how they should vote thereon.

The prevailing belief at that time was that a reserve fund was not necessary for the safety and perpetuity of the Endowment institution. This belief was largely based on the delusion that the *"infusion of young blood,"* the addi-

---

aber wie kann die Ausführung der Wittwen- und Waisen-Unterstützung für die Zukunft bei zunehmender Sterblich-keit, ohne eine Ueberbürdung der Brüderschaft, sicherge-stellt werden."- *Report D. G. L. No.* 1, 1872, *page* 91.

9. See Reports of D. G. L. No. 1, Nov. 24, 1872, page 126.

tion of new members in place of those lost by
death and withdrawal, prevents the advance in
age. It was supposed that the *average age* would
remain the same, and consequently the mortality
would not materially increase ; and that, even
should this slightly increase, our members would
always be willing and ready to pay the assessments required for the support of the widows
and orphans for their brethren. It was even
contended, by the opponents of a reserve fund,
that "as the membership grew, the per capita tax
would *decrease*," that "the more members came
in, the less would be required to be paid by each
member annually."

This delusion, long and often disproved, was
just then resurrected by a number of Mutual
Benefit and Assessment Life Insurance Associations, whose ascendancy was favored by numerous failures and a consequent wide-spread distrust of the regular Life Insurance Companies.
From but eight Mutual Benefit Organizations of
this kind, in 1867, they increased during the
flight of a few years until they were numbered
by hundreds, all claiming to furnish life-insurance at greatly reduced cost and without large
reserve fund. They were conducted under dif-

ferent systems, more or less faulty and imperfect, yet sustained by a membership of hundred thousands and were collecting and paying over to the widows and orphans of their respective members—who happened to die first—millions of dollars.[10]

Why should not our brethren have believed

---

10. With some few exceptions these associations were organized with purely charitable motives, and stimulated by a growing dissatisfaction with ordinary Life Insurance. The late Alex. Gardner, Secretary Beneficial Endowment Association, Washington, D. C., one of the ablest advocates of the Assessment plan, said in an address to the fourth Annual Convention of the National Mutual Benefit Associations:

"It may be said, without impropriety, that we in a great measure, without either chart or compass, drifted into existence...........We all know that forms of thought sweep over a country like a tidal wave, and Relief or Mutual Benefit Associations seem at this time to be in the ascendant...........As a matter of course, a large number will never amount to anything except to be chronicled as having had an existence and died." Many have died since then, and left a terrible, a warning record; some associations have continued to grow and flourish, but have done so only by making changes in their plans, as experience and sound philosophy have shown them the better way. What progress has been made in the growth and maturity of their ideas is best shown by the platform adopted at their last convention, held in October 1884, at Cincinnati. *See Note* I *to Part II of this article.*

that our death rate would remain as it was, at least for many, many years, and the average age never increase to any considerable extent? They did not take the trouble to think, much less to figure, *how* it would be possible that with advancing years the average age should remain the same. They had been told by good and trustworthy men that the rate of mortality in the *old* Masonic fraternity was now but a small fraction over one per cent.; that the oldest Life Insurance Companies in this country do *not* show much increase in their mortality rates.[11] These were facts, and facts were a better proof than mere theories and mathematical calculations that they could not understand.

Most people imagine every question con-

---

11. This phenomen could be easily explained by the excessive "lapses" (withdrawals) prevailing in those societies. It has been shown from their own reports that in the Masonic fraternity, out of an average membership of 373,634, the duration of membership was fourteen years, in the Order of Odd Fellows, out of an average membership of 259,000, in twenty-seven years, the average duration was only ten years, and in the Mutual Life Insurance Company of New York the average duration of a policy was six years only! etc.

nected with life insurance a very difficult mathematical problem, whilst in reality it requires nothing but mere common-sense to *know* that, as each year we are growing one year older, the additional new members to any society would have to be younger by just as many years as all the surviving members have grown older in the aggregate during the year, in order that the average age might remain the same. If out of one hundred members—the matter of age being immaterial—*one* die, the surviving ninety-nine members would at the end of the year, and in the aggregate, be ninety-nine years older. By adding a new member for the one lost by death; the *number* of members would again be the same, but to balance also the advance in age, this new member would have to be ninety-nine years younger than the one who died. This would scarcely be possible. By adding *eleven* members, however, *each* nine years younger, the ninety-nine years would again be gained, but there would then be hundred and ten members of the same average age as the original one hundred were one year before.

And this was exactly the case in our Order at that time, especially in the older districts, with many members quite advanced in years, and where the accession of many new lodges, with young members,[12] considerably retarded the advance of the average age.

That this would not, aye, could not continue for any length of time, was foreseen by our more intelligent and experienced members. In the history of every social organization there comes a time when it is impossible to increase its membership, and when not more new members will join than about enough to supply the places of those who die and withdraw.[13] But even had, or would, such increase in membership continue in the future, the death rate would nevertheless

---

12. The total membership of our Order was :

			Increase in.	Ann. per cent.
July 1868	8,802 members.			
Jan. 1870	10,343	"	1½ years=1541 or	11½ "
Jan. 1871	11,742	"	1 year =1399 or	13½ "
Jan. 1872	13,327	"	1 year =1585 or	13¼ "
Jan. 1873	14,851	"	1 year =1524 or	11½ "
Jan. 1874	15,997	"	1 year =1146 or	7¾ "

13. Most Assessment Insurance Associations assume that nine per cent. of their members would lapse annually, and that by replacing these also with younger members they would be able to maintain the average age.

increase, as *average* age is no true basis to the rate of mortality.[14]

Our lodges number upon their rolls a majority of men of more than ordinary intelligence, but few of these have leisure to devote to this subject; some of them are men of large business-enterprise, to whom individually the benefit of one thousand dollars is a matter of little concern; and while they admit that it is a subject of much importance to a large number of their brethren, they excuse themselves from any effort to enlighten them, on the ground that the very members who most need this benefit would neither listen nor meditate, but would rely on the small mortality now experienced,[15] on the glittering promises of some assessment-insurance agents, and would elect those only as their representatives to the Grand Lodge who would promise to work and vote against any increase of taxation.

14. For example: In an equal number of members aged 30 and 60 years, their *average* age being 45 years, the mortality would be at the rate of 17 in 1000, while at the age of 45 years the mortality should really be only 11 in 1000.

15. In 1873, District No. 1 had a mortality of 7 in 1000; District No. 4, 5 and 6 even less than 5 in 1000 members.

Although the proposed General Endowment Law was defeated by the Constitution Grand Lodge, in 1874, this defeat caused an agitation that began to shake the popular delusion. It not only led to the adoption of an Endowment plan in District No. 2, that 'made provision for the accommodation of a large reserve fund by a per capita taxation of $15 per annum,[16] and that was in all other respects similar to the law originally proposed by the Executive Committee, but it opened the way for a reform of the Endowment fund in every District.

The warning voice of the President of the Order, cautioning its members, that without re-

16. The Endowment law of District No. 2 provided for "an assessment of seventy-five cents at the death of a member, but said assessments shall never exceed the sum of $15, *per capita*, in any one year." This district then embraced 200 members, thus paying proportionately the same amount as would have been paid under an Endowment-law, embracing the entire Order, with its 16,000 members, paying ten cents at the death of a member. In either case the mortality, at 9 in 1,000, could safely be assumed to produce $15. Other Districts were very quick in adopting the limitation to $15, but did not provide for assessments large enough, in proportion to the number of their members, to produce that amount.

serve fund "the annual taxation must increase to such an extent that at no great distance of time its practical execution will cease"—awoke the brethren from their dreams concerning the safety of our system. The incontrovertible principle enunciated in the report of the Executive Committee, that "the Endowments of those who die early must be paid by those who live long," entirely dispelled the delusion of a constant mortality of *one* per cent.; for, as not a single member could be expected to live long enough to pay, at this rate, the one thousand dollars for himself, much less could he be expected to pay, besides (at the rate of $10 or less per annum), for those who would die early. And so the members began to see or to feel that their small payments were insufficient.

The time had come when measures for a proper reserve fund could have been successfully introduced into every district; in fact, it was a step generally expected to be taken by the Grand Lodges. But the majority of representatives lacked either the knowledge or the courage—perhaps both—to adopt such measures. They knew that a reserve fund was now demanded; they also knew that in order to accumulate a sum, adequate for the purposes intended, increased taxation would be necessary. They could not assent to the latter proposition, much less offer it for consideration. Had they not always spoken in favor of "the poor man," and opposed the accumulation of large funds as unnecessary and dangerous ? Had they not even pledged themselves to work and vote against every increase of taxation ? An Endowment system, similar to the one adopted by District No. 2, would necessitate an annual contribution of $15, nearly double the sum paid by the members of their own district, and would be disliked by their Lodges. They doubted the success of the plan which District No. 2 had adopted. At all events, it would be safest to wait and see how it worked there, and they concluded, in their wisdom, that it behooved them, as prudent and careful legislators, to adopt *a reserve fund, of some kind, without imposing any additional burden* on the members. This would be popular ! Would it be sufficient. They knew little and cared less.

In District No. 1, the W. and O. Endowment Committee recommended (on July 26th, 1874) the establishment of a reserve fund to be

constituted from the accumulation of small surplus amounts above the sum of $1,000, received
in the collection of assessments (@ 16 cts.) at
the death of a member. This "surplus" then
amounted to $8,406.75, and to it was to be ad-
ded such surplus as was derived from each
future assessment, together with the interest on
its investment. At the end of five years, Endowments should be paid out of this fund whenever
the number of deaths exceeded the ratio of *one*
per cent. of the brethren of said District. The
said committee at the same time recommended
that the rate of assessments be *reduced* from time
to time, so that the Endowment plan would be
economic, yet consistent with the safety of this
benefit.[17]

---

17. The following, copied from the said official report
(1874–75, pp. 91, 92), is characteristic: "As to the establishment of a Sinking or Reserved Fund it must be apparent
to the Grand Lodge that in order to insure the payment of
the $1,000, *and to secure* brethren from onerous assessment
which may arise by a large and sudden increase in the death
rate, owing to epidemic or general disaster (!?) some measure looking to the formation of a Reserved Fund should be
adopted. Your Committee therefore present to the consideration of the Grand Lodge the following plan of a Reserved Endowment Fund, which, it is hoped, will meet the
demands of the District."

"The object in view is *not* the amassing of a large fund,

This recommendation was adopted at the Grand Lodge session of 1875.

The immediate result of this law was, that, in 1876, the rate of Endowment Assessments was reduced to fifteen cents, although in the preceding year the full amount paid by each member was merely $7.20. In 1877, it was further reduced to fourteen cents, and in 1879 to thirteen and a half cents, thus, up to December 31, 1878, producing a reserve-fund of only $44,757.-38 with a membership of 8,495, of whom more than four hundred were above the age of sixty, some of them over seventy years of age. In the face of these facts the Grand Lodge members, in charge of this fund, continually spoke of its "growing magnitude," and while they admitted that the Reserve-fund would become a necessity, if the institution was to be a permanent one, and should be increased as much and as rapidly as possible—they did not propose an increase of the Endowment tax.[18]

-----

to burden the brethren, but a sure and gradual accumulation, and it is herewith recommended that the Endowment rate be *reduced* from time to time, so that it will be economic, at the same time consistent with the safety of this benefit."

18. See Report of the W. and O. Reserve fund Com-

DISTRICT No. 6, the progressive District, ever going "onward," was the first to establish a sinking fund in connection with its Endowment plan. This was done as early as 1869, but also without making any provision for its revenue, with the exception of "voluntary contributions, donations, legacies, etc ," to which at a later date were added "the proceeds of the per capita tax for the Endowment-fund, in excess of the $1,000, to be paid into the sinking fund."

In 1874, the General Committee, in its official report to the Grand Lodge, wrote : " The sinking fund was created by the Endowment, and ought by law to be used for no other than Endowment purposes. We have evidence before us from a mathematician who has worked, and now works, for Insurance Companies as actuary, that without reserve we cannot exist,[19] and

---

mittee, Jan 25th, 1871.—*Proceedings D. G. L. No.* 1 *p.* 63.

19. Every authority on Life-insurance will confirm this. Numerous testimony to the same effect, obtained from about twenty experts was published in the Chicago *Tribune* of May 6, 1880. *Cornelius Walford*, of London, England, an acknowledged authority on Life-insurance, wrote :

"I confess I have looked with amazement at the development—I will rather say, the craze—which has set in for the

this reserve is in our Endowment sinking
fund." The committee, therefore, recommended that the taxation be eighty cents, which,
with 1500 members, would amount to $1200,
leaving a surplus of $200 for the sinking fund.

But this was dissented from by the Grand
Lodge members, and the committee, to whom
that report was referred, commented thereon as
follows :......" This new idea, debated upon in
all Lodges, and condemned in many instances,
is the creation of a large Reserve fund, to provide for emergencies in cases of epidemics or
other unforeseen causes.[20]   The establishment

promulgation of schemes of this sort with you, during the
last ten years or so.   My amazement consists in this, that
whereas I am accustomed to give credit to those who reside
on your soil (referring to the United States) for having a
large degree of sagacity, yet in this particular matter they
appear to have shown literally none, but rather to have put
a blind faith in the impossible ''

Dr. *Karl Heym*, the celebrated German mathematician
wrote in his report, made at the request of *Bismarck* (who
favored the introduction of some cheap insurance plan for
the working men), as follows :

"Unless these funds, required by the principles of life-
insurance, are provided, societies of this class do far more
harm than good, and they visit the sins of the founders
upon generations that come after them."

20.   The leading members and strongest advocates of

of these funds is an imitation of the Re-insur-
ance Reserves of Insurance Companies, to provide for a time when no new business can be

_____

Co-operative, or rather of Assessment insurance without
large reserve funds, always insisted on the necessity of providing for a Contingent or Reserve-fund, to insure the safety
of these associations in case of excess of deaths from any
cause.

Fred. H. Waldron, representing the Masonic Mutual
Benefit Association of New Haven, Conn., and Recording
Secretary of the Mutual Benefit Associations' Convention,
held at Washington, D. C., in 1879, said in his essay, full
of excellent arguments on this question :

"I must confess that before giving this subject much
serious thought, I was not in favor of accumulating a fund,
but the more I studied this phase of these Associations, the
more 1 became convinced that a reserve fund was essential
to their life and stability, and I think, during the experience
of our Association, that we will find a surplus necessary in
the event of a sudden excess of death."

And at the close of his arguments he comes to the conclusion that for such Associations (with properly graded
assessments) "All that is required is : enough to meet any
contingency in case of an excess of deaths from any cause.
I should advocate the accumulation of from $15 to $20 for
each member on the rolls. An Association of 2,000 members, with a surplus of from $30,000 to $40,000, would, in
my mind. meet the contingency."

And the Committee of that Convention of Mutual Benefit
Associations, consisting of the Representatives of Assess

obtained by them any more, or their income should fall below their expenditures. Our Endowment fund cannot and should not be com-

---

ment Insurance exclusively, and to whom the subject of "Endowment Reserve funds" was referred, reports:

"That in their opinion a Reserve or Sinking fund is imperatively necessary and essential. If our Associations are to guarantee any payment in the future, there should be a foundation, a basis, in short, a fund to draw from in hours of distress, epidemic, or any other emergency. The question of cheap insurance can only receive permanency by having a reserve fund.

"We therefore recommend that each Association should hold in reserve an amount equal to twenty losses, and thus be provided for any contingency that may arise."

Since that time, as Assessment Insurance has advanced in experience and knowledge, the National Convention of Mutual Benefit Associations has made it a condition of membership, and a standard for distinguishing the sound from the unsound, the honest from the fraudulent plan, that it must have "either rates increasing with the advancing age of the insured or a fund in lieu of increasing rates."

The problem of Life-insurance without large reserve funds, in other words, of eliminating the Savings bank element from Life-insurance, has occupied the minds of the best actuaries, and the only conclusion to which they came, or could come, was, that it is impossible, except by rates increasing with age. How this would work, will be hereafter shown in this study. Here only reference will be made to the words of *Sheppard Homans*, one of the first actuaries of our times, and the leading advocate of Life Insurance *without*

pared to Insurance Companies. Our Order is in itself a Mutual Society bound together by a voluntary contract, whose observance is essential to membership therein. We may declare right here, with a sense of security, that the existence of the Order is no chimerical idea, but is secured beyond peradventure. Those members who are called away into the Great Grand Lodge above, are replaced by younger members, who thereby become the Reserve fund of the Endowment fund. The resources of our Endowment fund, looking at it from an Insurance standpoint, are fifty times that of a well regulated Life Insurance Company. Every individual member of this District represents a Reserve–fund of $1,000, on which fund you can draw as often as the case may require, and will always find a response, notwithstanding panics or other financial disturbances. This, with a membership of 1500, would give us a Reserve fund of

large accumulations: "A Life Insurance Society," he says, "must be compensated each year for the insurance furnished, for expenses of management, *and for possible adverse contingencies* ......*Beyond this* a reserve or deposit is not necessary, and is not always desirable."

one and a half millions, a very respectable sum for the few policies (so to say) issued."

This committee proposed that the rate of assessment be reduced to the "pro-rata ratio of the whole membership to the sum of $1,000, but shall not be made in fractions less than five cents," thus leaving almost nothing to be added to the sinking fund. It further recommended that the "Sinking Fund" be changed to a "Reserve fund," out of which Endowments shall be paid in cases of emergency.

Thus some shallow, glittering phrase, flattering to a popular delusion, will—for a short time —defeat the voice of truth, of science, and of common-sense. But soon the agitation rose again ; soon the voice of reason was again heard. The message of the General Committee to the Convention of District Grand Lodge No. 6, held January 2, 1877, at Detroit, Mich., submitted the following timely remark : "If we concede that within a period of forty years nine-tenths of our (*surviving*) members will have passed their seventieth year, we can easily conclude that in course of time the Endowment assessments must become quite heavy and burdensome." And the report of the Endowment Committee on the

same question furnishes further testimony as to
the eagerness felt for reconstructing their Endowment plan on a sounder basis.[21] Accompany-
ing that report was a resolution : " That the
President of the Grand Lodge appoint a com
mission of five members of the Grand Lodge,
as a *Committee on Endowment,* to act conjointly
with the Board of Trustees, which commission
is charged with the duty of organizing for
active and earnest work during the vacation, to
gather statistics and report to this convention
such details as will perfect our present Endowment Law." This commission prepared quite

---

21. A few brief extracts from this report may be interesting:

"In the original discussion on the establishment of this
scheme, many prophecies were uttered, which have since
proven to be correct. It was then emphasized that without
a strong reserve fund the scheme was a delusion; but we
groped our way in the dark, uninstructed through our own
perverseness, until now the experience of the past teaches
us to look well to this matter and organize a system which
will be a blessing to those who helped to perfect it...........
We again hear the pious wish of increasing the Endowment,
of decreasing the Assessments; and the air is full of the discussion, which marks the discourse between the eloquent
insurance solicitor and the intended victim.........Charity
loses none of its virtue because it uses the multiplication
table, and studies the science of figures."

a pamphlet, containing all the Endowment Laws of our different districts, some statistics, a reprint of a paper by the author of this study, published in 1872 (and used it without consulting him or giving him an opportunity to correct or perfect the same!), besides a proposed Endowment Law, which followed the main features of the law in District No. 2. In conclusion of its report, the Commission said, "We trust that the plan so successfully practiced in the Second District, will be adopted by the Grand Lodge.

The adoption of this plan will give us a permanent Reserve fund......To carry on the levying of small assessments, is a snare on a majority of the members, and only those would reap the benefit of an Endowment, whose decease would occur within the next ten or twenty years. If we wish to build a permanent Endowment, let us build wisely.

There might have been a chance for the adoption of the plan, had not this pamphlet first been transmitted for discussion to the Lodges, where it again met the cant of deluded brethren in favor of the popular delusion, the senseless schemes of cheap Life Insurance, (promulgated by the "Protective Life" of Chicago, the "Mutu-

al Protection Life" of Philadelphia and similar
companies), and where there are so few members
who understand the first principles of this
science. And still there might have been a
chance for its adoption, had said commission
taken a firmer stand before the Convention, had
it been earnest and well prepared to defend the
plan it recommended, instead of bestowing ful-
some praise on the author of this plan "who for
years had given the subject his best thoughts"—
and whose self-same plan they lightly abandoned, yielding to propositions to which they had
never before given the least consideration.

In January, 1878, at the Tenth Annual Convention of District Grand Lodge No. 6, the Report of said Endowment Commission, and its
supplementary report—recommending that each
Lodge be the custodian of its own reserve [22] at
only three per cent. interest—together with a
large number of other propositions, were referred, as usual, to an Endowment Committee,
which reported as follows :

"The future prosperity and welfare of our

_____

22. The working of this method will be shown in the
progress of this study.

District demand that we recognize the protection which this system offers—in failure of which we would be guilty of inexcusable selfishness and criminal neglect......A solemn and moral obligation presses upon us to maintain that indemnity. In view of these considerations we unhesitatingly recommend to this Convention the adoption of the declaration prefacing the proposed law, which reads: 'The Endowment scheme is hereby declared an integral part of the Constitution of District Grand Lodge No. 6, and a Reserve fund is hereby declared to be an indispensable part of the Endowment scheme, upon whose integrity, increase and constant support, the existence of a permanent Endowment scheme is dependent.' " And yet this very report recommended "the adoption of sections 1, 2 and 3, substituting therein an assessment of sixty cents instead of seventy-five cents, and $12 instead of $15," thus destroying the very basis of the necessary Reserve fund. It further recommended the adoption of the proposition which places the Reserve in the custody of the various Lodges, fixing the rate of interest at three per cent.[23]

23. To appreciate the difference produced by the rate

A long, excited discussion ensued. Every motion was lost. Finally the President declared that the Convention's test vote is opposed to the change of the present law.

It would exceed the scope of this study, and would overtax the patience of the reader, to fully review the discussions, struggles and troubles about our Endowments in every District[24]—excepting:

---

of interest it must be considered that $1, improved at compound interest, will amount in fifty years, at three per cent., to $4.38, while at six per cent. it will amount to $18.42.

24. DISTRICTS No. 3 and 4 have no Endowment Reserve fund to this day ; DISTRICT No. 5 seemed to have considerable trouble about delinquent Lodges, and some agitation with regard to abolishing the Reserve fund established in 1874, and held by and under the control of each Lodge. This Endowment-sinking fund of District No. 5 was founded on a basis of fifteen cents per member, paid with each assessment to the Trustees of their respective Lodge, each Lodge having control of its own accumulation, and "all assessments over twenty deaths shall be paid from this fund." The defects of this plan will be considered with the further development of our Endowment institution *after* the Constitutional Convention in 1879. DISTRICT No. 7, which separated from its mother, eager for the Endowment boon, and which during the first year of its working (in

DISTRICT No. 2. Considering that the Endowment plan of this District was the only one which provided for the accumulation of what the other Districts considered—"a large Reserve," and for assessments amounting to $15 annually, which were deemed "excessive and oppressive"—an examination of its working and progress is important.

Inaugurated in 1874, after long and violent opposition, and under serious difficulties, its success was doubted at first, but the opposition was checked, the difficulties overcome; the Law was sustained by our Court of Appeals and by the civil courts; it received the prompt compliance of all the Lodges of the District and the cheerful support of the members, including most of its former opponents.

In January, 1875, the President, in his Message to the first annual Grand Lodge meeting after its adoption, remarks: "The unusually large at-

1873) experienced fourteen deaths in one month out of only 853 members—preferred to increase the benefit from $1,000 to $1,500 rather than to provide for such emergencies in the future, by any reserve-fund except the initiation fee of $2.00 from each member, which amount does certainly not deserve that name.

tendance at said special meeting (held at Cincinnati, March 1, 1874) fully illustrated the intense
interest of the District in the important legislation about to take place. The Endowment Law
passed at said meeting is undoubtedly the best
and perhaps the only safe Endowment Law of
any now in existence in the various Districts of
our Order."

In January, 1876, the President of the District
Grand Lodge—an able opponent of the Endowment system and to the amassing of large funds
in benevolent associations—reports that "the
Endowment seems to be giving general satisfaction throughout the district." The committee,
to whom the second annual report of the Endowment-fund was referred, unanimously reported: "We take great pleasure in congratulat-
ing the District Grand Lodge upon the successful operation of the Endowment Law, and are
pleased to note that every Lodge in the District
cheerfully complies with the enforcement of the
Law."

In January, 1877, the President's Message
says: "The Endowment continues to give
general satisfaction, and to fulfil the object for
which it was originally intended." And the un-

animous report of the Committee on the Third Annual Report of Endowment-fund Trustees, says : "The smooth and effective workings of the law during the past year affords ample matter for congratulation. The sympathetic co-operation of the Lodges, manifested by the marked promptness in their duties, evidences not only the popularity of the Law, and the effectiveness of its charity, but that the little opposition, which still survives among a few unfortunate members, is, if not purely factious, at least undeserving the attention of this Grand Grand Lodge other than what is due to it out of respect for the courts of law of our country. We agree with the Trustees in their suggestion "that no change of the plan and system of our Endowment-fund is desired or advisable." "We feel satisfied that the present law is about as free from imperfections as any probable amendments could possibly make it. We believe that if we, this year, 'let well enough alone,' we shall certainly be guilty of a wisdom which will not only be appreciated by our constituents, but which will also afford a bright example to our own members and our successsors."

In January 1878, the President, in his annual message, said: "Lodges have promptly and cheerfully complied with the provisions of the Endowment Law, and its working has developed the wisdom of its plan in establishing and maintaining a reserve-fund based upon correct principles........Mathematical truths cannot be controlled by our wishes, endowments must be received before they are paid out, though the advocates of many plans seek to evade the axiom by pretensions of 'cheap insurance'....While objections are frequently raised to the formation of a large reserve fund, they are answered by its necessity. Provision must be made for the naturally increasing rate of future mortality, if we would not witness all the benefits absorbed by members dying at an early period, and none remain for those dying later." The Committee on the Endowment Trustees' Report, (the fourth year) again unanimously expressed "congratulation for the smooth and effective working last year." Nevertheless a majority of that committee desired the repeal of Section 17 of that Law, referring to the mode of amending the same.

---

25. One of the great bulwarks of this Endowment Law is this Section 17, which provides that all proposed amend—

In January 1879, the President speaks in his
Message of the prosperity of the District in
géneral only; but the Committee to whom was
referred the fifth annual report of the Endowment Fund Trustees, unanimously agreed that
...."it would be folly to permit or to advise any
material changes in our Endowment Law, after
having seen the proof of the excellence of the
system and method adopted in District No. 2,
and we recommend to this Grand Lodge to let
well enough alone, and to entertain no propo·
sition tending to disturb the peaceful opera·

---

ments must be referred, first to the Board of Trustees, and,
if recommended by a majority of its members, shall then
be submitted to the Grand Lodge for its action. This provision, which precluded even the discussion of all unsound
and unwise charges, was persistently attacked during the
first years of its action, but the firmness of the framers of
this Endowment law, the general satisfaction which it gave,
the confidence in the Board of Trustees, successfully defeated every attempt to repeal or modify this provision.
One member of the above-mentioned committee made a
minority report with regard to this matter of repealing section 17, saying: "I deem the recommendation (to repeal
Section 17) unwise and injurious to the best interests of the
institution;" and this minority report was adopted by a
vote of forty-one against twenty

tions of this well matured law........The re-
markably small percentage of lapses is no less
a subject for gratification, and speaks volumes
in favor of our system as compared with those
charitable societies that rejuvenate their member·
ship by crowding out the older members and
soliciting the young."

It should be noticed that the foregoing quotations are *not* from the reports of the Endowment
Fund Trustees, who might be supposed to present the condition and working of the institution
under their charge in a too favorable light.
They are the unbiassed official expressions of
the Grand Lodge Presidents and Committees
that, in this District, were changed every year.

Figures and facts may, however, give another
proof of the successful working of the Endowment Law of District No. 2.

During the quinquennial period, now under
review—namely, from the General Convention
of our Order in 1874 to that in 1879—the *increase in membership* in District No. 2, though
much less than that in the younger Districts,
though less attractive to that element which
might have joined for the sake of cheap insurance only, was fully equal to the increase in

District No, 1 (23 per cent.), and larger than that in District No. 3, whose members pay no tax for a reserve fund.

The annual *lapses* in District No. 2 (1½ to 2 per cent.) were less than before the adoption of the Endowment Law, by far less than in other fraternal organizations, and not above the rate of lapses in other districts of our Order. This clearly proves that a taxation necessary to the safety and perpetuity of our Endowments is neither detrimental to the increase in membership nor does it cause members to withdraw; on the contrary, it produces *confidence*, a powerful magnet. And "the poor men" are those who complain least about paying at the rate of five cents per day to *secure* the Endowment to their family.

The rate of mortality in District No. 2 was greater than either in District No. 1, or No. 6, especially in the years 1876 and 1878, when it reached fully one per cent. In District No. 1 this per centage was reached for the first time in 1879. During those two years ten endowments ($10,000) were paid out of the reserve funds of District No. 2 ; so far none were paid out of he reserve funds of the other districts. Never-

theless, at the end of 1878(the fifth year) the reserve fund of District No. 2 amounted to $55,-
794, or over $20 per member, while in District
No. 1 at the same time it amounted to $44,757,
or but little over $5.00 per member.[26]

As for the safety of these accumulations, the
following pithy remark in the sixth annual report may answer : "The best evidence of the
excellent condition of our Reserve-fund is the
prompt payment of interest at maturity, and that
even those few investments on Real Estate
Mortgage, which, by circumstances, had to be
foreclosed, brought *more* than our claim from
principal, interest and costs. Not one is in arrears.
The Treasurer's report gives the investments
in detail with names of the parties' mortgages,
and the investigating committee may easily inform itself as to the value of the securities."
And as to the *cost of management*, the same report shows that "all this has been accomplished

---

26. In the excellent articles on " The Problem of the
Orders' by FRATERNAL *(American Hebrew—Vol.* 19) it
was shown that on Jan. 1, 1884, the Reserve-fund of District No. 2 represented four and a half per cent. of the
amount assured, whilst that of District No. 1 represented
only one and a half per cent. of that amount.

without disputes or complications, at the merely nominal expense of 33 cents per year for each $1,000 insured. Not a single Lodge is in arrears; not a single appeal is brought; not a murmur of discontent or suspicion is heard ; confidence in the management and permanence of our Endowment-fund is almost unanimously expressed."

The fears, often expressed by the opponents of a Reserve fund plan, have been silenced in this district, and are no less unfounded in every other district of our Order. The very men who would distrust the chosen trustees of their own brethren, insure with companies holding millions of such trust-funds, and of whose managers they know nothing whatever. Proper control and checks should, of course, be established ; [27] but

---

27. The Trustees of the Endowment-fund of District No. 2 have themselves made this remark in one of their reports:" The growing magnitude of your fund demands, and your Board of Trustees desires and invites the closest scrutiny of their doings and accounts. Committees generally examine but hastily and superficially. But our Endowment fund system, with its uniform assessments and benefits, is so simple, and our Secretaries tables are so well arranged, that each Lodge can examine for itself and verify our report."

these are provided for in *every* Endowment-law, however defective it may otherwise be, and none of our Districts have ever had cause to complain of any default of its managers ; hundreds of thousands of dollars have passed through their hands, and not a cent has been lost. The same may also be said of the trustees of our sister organizations, with one single exception, and there the loss was small ; the sureties made good the deficiency as far as they were liable, and in that single exceptional case the proverb might, perhaps, be applied : "Like master, like man."

Another fact, indicating the successful working of the Endowment-plan of District No. 2, and the satisfaction with its management, was the re-election, with nearly every year, of those members of its Board of Trustees, whose term had expired.[28]

---

28. In 1879 the author of this study, whose term as Trustee then expired, assured the Grand Lodge that he preferred the election of some one else in his place ; were it only to assure themselves that the satisfactory and prosperous condition of their Endowment-fund would not be endangered, nor the continuance thereof interrupted by any change of its managers, so long as its present system was strictly adhered to, and the sound principles on which it

But although the excellence of the plan and method, adopted in District No. 2, had been commended by its own Grand Lodge, as well as by those of other Districts, these facts were but little known to the Lodges. Consequently it also was of but little avail that the Executive Committee, in its report for 1878, published a treatise on the subject of "Fraternal Insurance," which fully explained the questions involved, and the calculations for a proper Reserve, required under various circumstances as to rate of interest and age of members.

Unfortunately our Order has no organ whereby such information, in popular form and small doses, could be brought home to large numbers

---

was based would be observed. But the Committee on Endowments unanimously reported as follows: "There is a provision, not incorporated in our statutes, but written in the heart of every brother of our District, which has made Bro. Isidor Bush the *Abuo ben Adhem* of this District—*an officer for life of the institution*—which by his energy and foresight, his patience and perseverance, has been devised, established and continued upon a sound basis." And this was demonstrated to be the unanimous feeling of the Grand Lodge, in so touching and enthusiastic a manner that he feels in duty bound to serve the cause to the best of his
. ability, as long as his strength will permit.

of its members. Thus the greater majority of our brethren in blissful ignorance continued to be pleased with the working of their (cheap) Endowment-plans, or, at most, lamented the increased mortality experienced from year to year· And though they gradually began to see that, to secure the stability of the Endowment system, to save it from the calamity of failure, or its proving a fraud, some better plan would have to be resorted to —there was then, as yet, very little prospect for its general adoption

The Constitution Grand Lodge of our Order held its third quinquennial General Convention in the city of Philadelphia on January 26th, 1879, and remained in session five full days. Its work was of an important character, and, considering the unwieldy body, much was accomplished. But it did nothing to solve the problem of *"Our Endowments,"* nothing "to give stability and permanence to this mode of supporting the widows and orphans of our deceased brethren."

The President, in his message to the Convention, declared this the all-important point to be kept in view. He hoped that, having called attention to the needed modifications, and the District Grand Lodges having full power to en—

act such laws, they would "be encouraged to strengthen their several Endowment plans by wise legislation, to make them permanently successful, so as to keep faith with the promises and expectations held out to their members."

The Lodges of San Francisco, District No. 4, transmitted a memorial through their delegates, wherein they said that at the last Constitutional Convention (in 1874) an effort to establish a "General Endowment" system was fortunately frustrated; and fearing that the advocates of the "injudicious measure" might renew their attempt in that direction, they therefore petitioned the Convention to refrain from the passage of any law altering the present status of the Endowment system.

Resolutions adopted by Lodges of other Districts, protesting against any changes of their Endowment Laws, were also submitted, and many representatives were instructed by their Lodges, among them even Mount Sinai No. 270, the largest Lodge in our Order, "to oppose a national Endowment Law" and to leave each District to work out its own destiny.[29] District

29. As per printed Reports to Excelsior Lodge No. 170,

Grand Lodge No. 7 was the only one that presented a memorial in favor of a General Endowment plan. This plan was accompanied by a proposed law which assumed to secure fifteen hundred dollars to the widow, orphans or other beneficiaries of every member, by assessments of $1.00, to be repeated as often as the fund would have been reduced to such an amount as to preclude paying the next death–claim. No provision whatever was herein made for a reserve-fund to meet either a possible excess of deaths by epidemics[30] or other calamity, or for the certain increase of mortality in future years.

It was quite natural, therefore, that the Endowment Committee of that Constitution Grand Lodge, far from cherishing any desire to renew its misjudged attempts of the preceding Convention (in 1874) reported as it did ; namely : "That we deem it against the wishes of a majority of the fraternity and of the various Districts, as well as inexpedient *at this time*, to enact a general Endowment Law."

------

and to Mount Sinai Lodge No. 270, by their respective delegates.

30. And this District had lost sixty-one members

"We do most earnestly recommend, however, that the various Districts endeavor to improve their laws—as recommended in his report by the worthy President of the Executive Committee to this Constitution Grand Lodge—"keeping constantly in view the all-important point to give stability and permanence to this mode of supporting the widows and orphans of our deceased brethren, and to keep faith with all our members."

"This cannot be done without *either* accumulating an adequate Reserve-fund, *or* raising each member's contributions as he arrives at ages in which the rate of mortality naturally increases. [31]

---

through yellow fever, and that during a few weeks (August-October) of the year then (1878) just closed.

31. A proposition "that assessments, wherewith to pay the Endowment benefits to widows and orphans upon the decease of a member, shall be levied, varying in accordance with the age of each member at the time of joining the Order," was submitted to the General Committee of D. G. L. No. 1, but was not considered " *as the General Convention might take this matter in consideration.*" But this matter has been carefully considered by the ablest advocates of Assessment-insurance. These have soon recognized the weakness and unfairness of plans which charged young and old with the same amounts at each assessment—while the principles of

And as the latter method would become very
burdensome to our older members and cause
many of them to withdraw, we recommend, AS A

equity required that members, during the probable life of
each, should pay like sums for like benefits. If a member,
who is twenty-eight years old, and has an expectancy of
thirty six years, pays assessments of $1.00 at each death,
another member, who is thirty-eight years old, having an
expectancy of not quite twenty-nine years, should pay $1.25,
and a member, fifty-three years of age, who has an expectancy of eighteen years, should evidently pay $2.00 on
each assessment. Hence many Mutual Benefit Associations
have graded assessments according to expectancy at the age
of joining. But they are mistaken in considering this plan
safe without proper reserve fund. These rates of assessments, though very fair, and not burdensome in the begin
ning, greatly increase in number, as the mortality increases
with the advancing age of the old members, and new members will not join. Why should they burden themselves
with the extra deaths occurring among those who have long
been members? That the latter have been paying into the
institution for many years, have already paid a large amount
into its treasury, and have taken out nothing, is of no benefit to future members—since it has all been paid out again
for death-claims, and nothing reserved to offset the increasing liabilities arising from the advancing age of members.
Furthermore, rates graded according to age at the time of
admission, and remaining unchanged thereafter, must soon
result in unequal assessments on members of equal age. A
member, for instance, whose age at joining is twenty-eight,

NECESSITY, the establishment of adequate Reserve-funds, properly invested and guarded, sufficient to provide with equal justice for all our

---

would in ten years (when thirty-eight years old) still pay only $1.00 Assessments, whilst one of the same age (thirty-eight), who may then desire to join, would be charged $1.25. He would protest; he would say: "It is unjust that I should pay more than another of the same age; that this other entered ten years back, makes him no better risk; on the contrary, his health may be impaired; for what he paid, he had his equivalent, his insurance all the time; he paid nothing for me or for my benefit; aye, he would have to continue paying over seventy years longer at the same rate, if he lived that long, to pay enough for his own benefit." Nor is the system of rates, graded according to age of entry, as equitable as some suppose. Out of 1,000 men aged twenty-one to thirty, there will occur after ten years (when their ages will be between thirty-one to forty) about *one* death more annually than during the preceding decade, while among men aged forty-five at entry, the mortality will increase, in ten years, at the rate of about one out of 100 members, and then continue rapidly increasing. Thus it will be seen that the number of assessments is chiefly increased by the rapid growth of the death-rate among the old men. But as all, young as well as old, must contribute for each death, the system is not quite equitable; and, under it, new, young members would certainly not join, if they understood that they must share in paying for the greater increase in the death-rate of the old members.

members, and guarding against their contributions ever becoming too burdensome by an excessive mortality, either from epidemics or through the natural decline of life in future years." etc.

*   *   *   *   *   *   *

"Nevertheless your committee does *not* recommend that this Constitution Grand Lodge exercise its supreme legislative power in prescribing limits of benefit or other rules to the various Districts on the subject of Endowments, hoping that the Grand Lodge may enact such wise laws for the protection of the widows and orphans as will conduce to the welfare of their sections. But we cannot refrain from expressing the con-

---

Recognizing these defects the National Convention of Mutual Benefit Associations has adopted the rule that "If the mortality rates do not increase with age, after entry, the rates at entry must be loaded twenty-five per cent., at five per cent. per annum, compound interest, and such loading with interest must be held as a liability or reserve." (The Chicago Guaranty Fund Life Society, which works under this system, provides for a guaranty fund of one million dollars, and besides for a reserve-fund raised from a large percentage deducted from the benefits of those members who die during the first five years of their member - ship

viction that a more correct and more uniform system and method in the several Endowment plans of all the Districts is very desirable, and would promote the best interests of the members and the strength and beauty of our Order."

Three members of said Endowment Committee made a minority report, stating that in their judgment *the only secure basis for the maintenance of the Endowment was to make it general.* But "being aware that a majority of this Convention was opposed to any change, they deemed it a useless waste of time to present any plan for consideration."

The Convention adopted the report of the majority of the committee.

With this decision of the Convention, to let each District work out its own destiny, a new period in the history of our Widow and Orphans Endowments began. A period, alas! of struggles, more violent, but no less futile, all awakened by proposed changes in the Endowment laws of the various Districts ; struggles between those who desired to secure the system from failure with its fatal consequences, and those who desired the greatest benefits for the smallest contributions; between those who wanted insurance which assures, and those who want it for half cost, or less; between the young lodges who figured how much they had already paid for the benefit of the old lodges,[32] and for this reason

———

32. In the valuable articles on "The Problem of the Order," by FRATERNAL (in the *American Hebrew*) it was shown that the "six of the old Lodges of District No. 1 already received (up to 1884) nearly $117,000 more in Endowments paid to their members than they paid to the fund—while nine of the younger Lodges paid nearly $85,000 more than they received—which will also soon be eaten up by the older Lodges. How long can such a condition of affairs last?"

Compare with this the condition of affairs in District No. 2. There also during the eleven years, from 1874 to 1885, notwithstanding that the annual contribution of every member has been $15, six of the old Lodges have received $18,900 more in Endowments paid to their members than these Lodges paid to the fund. But the interest accumulated during the same time amounts to $53,583.30, or nearly three times the excess paid for Endowments of members of these old Lodges. And not one cent had to be taken from the surplus of the younger Lodges who have paid in $150,-000 more than thay have received, but whose reserve fund now amounts to over $170,000 for only 3070 members. Had a General Endowment plan, based on the same principles, been adopted by all the Districts in 1874, their reserve fund would now, in the aggregate, amount to over

meditate secession, and the old lodges who did not figure or meditate at all ; between those who put their trust in a strong reserve fund, and those who trusted to nobody ; between those who wished to secure beyond doubt an Endowment for the poor brother's widow and orphans, and those who pretended to protect "the poor man " by saving him from paying the few additional cents which would be required for that purpose.

Endless discussions, devoted to legislation upon this subject, consumed the time of the District Grand Lodges from year to year, and resulted—in nothing. Had they but had no result whatever ! But, alas, they not only caused " so great an agitation, in most of the Districts, as to overshadow nearly every other object of the Order, and threaten to seriously interfere with its progress and prosperity," but in some Districts they resulted in making the Endowment plans worse than they already were ; and when one Grand Lodge at last succeeded in passing a better Endowment Law, APPEALS, on the ground of some technical defects in the mode of its

$1,300,000, for our 25,000 members, protecting these, and joining young members from an oppressive increase of assessments in the future.

adoption, again defeated it. In another District quarrels between the Grand Lodge and some of its oldest Lodges led to the dissolution of the latter and to more appeals to our Court of Appeal.

All this naturally led to great dissatisfaction until a clamor arose against the Endowment system, a cry to make it optional, or even do away with it entirely. The members who raised this clamor, however, seem to have forgotten that it is one of the principles and first duties of our Order "to provide for, protect and assist the widow and orphan." They did not consider hat this cannot be done without taxing the members, and that taxation cannot be imposed without equal rights.

A review of these struggles and troubles, and —let us hope—of their permanent, successful solution by the Constitution Grand Lodge. which meets next week (March 1, 1885), shall form the third part of this study.

Part III.—A Study of its Plans: their Working, Defects, and the Remedy.

The first Grand Lodge meeting, after the adjournment of the General Convention of 1879, was that of District No. 7, held on May 11th, 1869, at Memphis, Tenn. In his message, the President (Bro. Samuel Ullman) reviewed the history of the past year with its terrible affliction during the fall months of 1878—the yellow fever plague, which alone took sixty-two of our beloved brethren from us, casting gloom upon the hearthstone of so many families. After a beautiful obituary notice of the departed brethren and an acknowledgment of the noble acts of living heroes of the plague, and of the brotherly aid obtained from the sister districts and lodges of our Order, which helped to dispel the seeming impenetrable gloom, he made the following suggestions as to "Our Endowments:"

"Since the failure of the adoption of a universal endowment scheme by the Constitution Grand Lodge for the Order at large, I have come to the conclusion that certain changes in the law

governing the same will be necessary, in order
that the object may be maintained for which it
is intended. The last epidemic has demonstrated
how arduous our burdens may become, how
difficult for many Lodges to discharge the solemn
duty towards our deceased brethren. I would,
therefore, recommend *that we lower our benefit to
$1000, and that we tax our members at the rate of
$1.50 per month*, to be collected monthly in ad-
vance by the secretary of each lodge, for the
payment of which every lodge shall be made
responsible."   .

He did not claim to be a learned mathematician—but in the goodness of his heart and in-
spired by an honest solicitude "to enable the
poor brother to maintain his good standing, as
well as to preserve the integrity of our Order,"
he *intuitively* recommended the best, the only
correct plan for the future. Then, however, followed the report of the Secretary of the District,
(Bro. M. Ulman) proposing another plan. He
had "critically examined the laws and workings
of 130 organizations of like nature," in order to
find a remedy. He could say that this District
had grown under his eye and partially under his
guidance. His report showed the entire insuffi-

ciency of the endowment laws of the District
(which had also been made and adopted *under
his guidance*); and in the same report he declared
that, had these laws been complied with by him,
no benefits whatever could have been paid, as the
District was bankrupt; 30 lodges would have been
forced out of existence, and not less than 1,000
members been suspended for non-payment, or
would have left without saying "with your
permission," but that he had saved the District
and redeemed its promises by altogether ignoring
its laws and substituting rules of his own, to suit
the emergency.

The difficulties he had to contend with were
enormous; there were neither funds nor was there
confidence. He procured the former and gradually re-established the latter, paying for the
death-claims of that one year 89 endowments at
$1500—and its other expenses, the large sum of
$134,000! All this is established beyond doubt
or dispute, in his long report, and the prompt and
sagacious action, his zeal and devotion, received
the deserved praise of the endowment committee
and of every lover of the Order.

Hence any plan proposed by him at that meeting, every change of the endowment law which

he would have recommended, would have been promptly adopted; a more favorable moment for the introduction of a sound and enduring system could not have been chosen. Had he fully understood the subject, had he been willing to accept good authority instead of examining "the laws and workings of 130 associations of like nature," and disregarding the warnings furnished by his own Constitution Grand Lodge ; had he but been willing to support the wise suggestion of his President of District No. 7; it would now have been a model Widow and Orphan Endowment institution, with a large Reserve fund to uphold it. But he was not in favor of reducing the benefit from $1500 to $1000; and while he *did* ask an annual contribution of $24, or taxation at the rate of $16 for the benefit of $1000, that being $1 more than was charged in District No. 2, he did *not* know or did not want to know that the rate of mortality and of interest on reserve are the all-important factors. This contribution-rate of $16 was based on the presumed necessity of providing for an epidemic, at least once in every six years. "What has occurred will occur again," seemed to him an unchangeable law of nature; and as 96 per mille had died during the preced_ ing six years, the average would be 16 deaths out of 1000 in any one year. What may not be needed in three or four years is sure to be needed in the fifth."¹ If that were true, this rate would not and could not be sufficient for the accumulation of any reserve fund to provide for the additional necessity created by an increasing mortality due to the advancing age of its members.

1.—In the Proceedings of the 7th Annual Convention of D. G. L No. 7, May, 1880, page 92, this is repeated more distinctly still. The late Endowment Fund Secretary says in his report: "This law was enacted to cover a *decade* of six years (!) upon the basis of mortality for the preceding six, twelve and eighteen years, where the average mortality has invariably been sixteen per thousand. , . . the law of average is based upon experience that what has occurred will occur again, and the lapse of time upon previous occasions may be considered as the lapse of time for coming occasions."

Understand this, whosoever can ! But as District No. 7 did not exist longer than seven years, and as before that time its lodges, under the jurisdiction of No. 2, had no more than 700 members, those statistics are, fortunately, only imaginary ones. From fall of 1878 to spring of 1885, (now) over six years have elapsed without epidemic disease, and we hope and trust that (for years to come) none may again visit the South.

Fortunately, it is not true. The mortality in the Southern States, and especially among their Israelites, is on an average but slightly in advance of that among men of the same ages in the North. The period of six years, from 1873 to 1878 inclusive, during which the yellow fever scourged that territory TWICE, was an exceptional case, and probably may never again occur in so short a period. Not *all* that has occurred will occur again ; laws of averages are not deduced from an experience of a few years or a small number of individuals.

But the plan and the endowment law adopted in District No. 7 was very defective in this respect : that the management of the surplus, produced by the annual contribution of $26 from each member, was left to the lodges, each keeping a small fractional part, and the investment thereof was restricted to U. S. Bonds at 4 per cent. Moreover, this contribution was too large a tax for many members.

In 1881 the President of the District already said in his message : " Different causes have the past year prevented the required accession, and one of the most prominent was the cry of heavy taxation. Various opinions exist as to the advisability of reducing the benefit from $1,500 to $1,000 (the same as existing in other Districts), and thereby reducing the taxation for this branch alone 33⅓ per cent."

In the E. F. secretary's report for that year we find that the reserve amounted to $32,039, of which only $15,900 were invested in U. S. Bonds and all the remainder lay idle in currency.[2]   In this report he advises the accumulation of an adequate reserve fund, admits "that no organization, with endowment features attached, can exist for any length of time without an adequate reserve ;" and yet he is inconsistent enough to "recommend that the dues to this endowment (of $1500) be, after July 1st, 1881, $5.25 per quarter instead of $6.50, as they are now."

During that year the District had decreased by 130 members ; the decrease was generally attributed to the heavy taxation ; and it may be possible, wrote the said secretary, that the reduction of the quarterly endowment dues from

---

2.—He says : "Lodges who have neglected to invest as provided by law, were admonished to invest, but—the admonition remained unheeded." Later developments showed that the Lodges did not have the currency, either—had expended it for other purposes or lost it.

$6.50 to $5.25 will have the desired effect (to remove the dissatisfaction).

And what did the Committee on Endowment report?

" Recognizing the opposition to the adoption of their (first) report,[3] and being fully convinced that it would be unsafe to permanently reduce the present endowment assessment" — they yielded to the pressure for its reduction for one

---

3.—The first report, withdrawn after very lengthy discussion, is highly interesting from an historical standpoint. The limited scope of this study admits of a brief extract only.

The report asks this " Most Honorable Body," the D. G.L., not to be too hasty in condemning what may seem contrary to preconceived notions and an unreasoning public clamor. The committee says: "We have become convinced that, unless the endowment be relegated to a secondary position, the gravest results may be expected at an early day. . . . Unfortunately the endowment feature of the Order has obtruded itself so far into our councils and has claimed so much of our consideration, that we have in a great measure lost sight of everything else. It is an axiom of mechanics that "the strength of anything is the strength of its weakest part," and the axiom applies with full force to us. The endowment—being the weakest part of our structure, the whole edifice is as weak as it. If it totters, we fall. To remedy this evil the committee recommended :

year to $5.00 per quarter, and recommended that
a special committee of seven be appointed to report to the next annual session of this Grand
Lodge a basis for the endowment that would render it as economical as possibly consistent with
safety and justice.

This report, reducing the endowment dues
from $6.50 to $5 per quarter was, of course,
adopted. Thus another year was lost, at the end
of which, when the Grand Lodge met again (in
May, 1882) that part of the President's Message
which concerned the endowment said: "It has,
from the very institution of the District, furnished the all-absorbing topic of our annual meetings,
and yet we stand to day as insecure as in 1878,
when the very existence of the District was endangered by the heavy mortality of that year."
* * * * "As experimenting on the human

---

1. To make the endowment optional. 2. To employ an
efficient insurance actuary to determine the lowest safe
assessment and reserve fund with which we can continue
our present benefit. 3. When such calculation is com-
pleted to promulgate to the Lodges the new basis arrived at.
And a number of other points, all well and wisely considered,
to place the endowment under a separate administration and
under sound financial rules.

body invariably results in injury, or loss of life, so will experiments with our Endowment bring about a like result—our very existence will be crippled or endangered. The report of the Secretary from July 1, 1881, when the reduction of the assessment went into operation for the six months ending January 1, 1882, shows that this experiment has already resulted in a deficit of $4,376.25, whilst we should have had an increase. At the same rate, a continuance of the experiment would enable the endowment to last just so long as a dollar remains in the Reserve—that is, about four years."

" We are confronted annually by improbable schemes and impossible theories, which result in the hasty enactment of laws as impracticable in their execution as they are dangerous to the permanency of the Endowment. It is, in my opinion, time that we should be guided by experience and discard inexperience."

* * * * " Do not let us promise what we cannot accomplish, but let us establish the Endowment upon such a basis as will render it secure now and for all time to come."

To arrive at such a basis,—both the President and the Committee on Endowment commended a work on Co–operative Insurance by the worthy Secretary of the District "as tending to com- pletely overthrow the popular delusions on the subject." Yet, strange to relate, the said com- mittee then submitted an endowment plan of which it is said in its report :4 " It is absolutely necessary for the safety of our plan that our ag- gregate membership increase at the rate of ten to twelve per thousand annually, and that the acces- sions, requisite to replace our losses and furnish this increase, be of younger material."

Evidently, the Committee did not know that an insurance plan computed with a view to ac- cession of future members, is both unsound and dishonest; unsound, as no permanently contin- ued increase of membership can be relied upon, and dishonest, as taking from future younger members an amount needed for the deficiency of the old members is not much better than stealing.

In view of the fact that after the epidemic of Jan 1st, 1879, the membership of the District was

4.—Report of Special Committee on Endowment, ap- pointed at Vicksburg, 1881, submitted and referred to Com- mittee on Endowment, May 18th, 1882, for codification, adopted as a law May 16th, 1882.—Proceedings ix. Annual Convention, D. G. L. No. 7, pp. 112-124.

2665, and on Jan. 1st, 1882, only 2380, a *decrease* of 285 in three years—it would seem incomprehensible that such a plan should be called SAFE, and should be recommended by the learned Secretary who himself wrote that "no matter how numerous the new admissions, they will not materially retard the gradual increase of mortality, until it reaches the maximum, and in proportion increases the taxation until *it* reaches the maximum, provided the organization will not have collapsed earlier."

However, the report of the Committee on Endowment was adopted; the sum of twenty-four dollars was established as the annual contribution from every member, and the Grand Lodge decided to submit to the members of the Lodges, prior to next annual convention, the question as to the amount of benefit, whether it should remain $1500, or be reduced to $1000.

The result of submitting this question was, that out of the 2334 contributing members (a further decrease of 46 members in about six months), 889 voted for $1,500 and 86 only for $1,000 (1359 members not voting), which was quite natural—especially as the learned Grand Secretary assured them that "our present laws contain no errors; they are as perfect as human heads can frame them."⁵ —[See Proceedings for 1882, page 24.]

In DISTRICT No 1, the agitation of the Endowment question—immediately after the adjournment of the B. B. Convention held in Philadelphia in January; 1879—became even more intense than in District No. 7; and its study may be found interesting and *especially instructive for the future solution of* this problem in that greater District of our Order.

Through the medium of the press, and even in public medium meetings, serious charges and unfriendly criticisms were freely indulged in. The message of the President of the District Grand Lodge session (Jan. 25th, 1880), in reviewing the past year, speaks of its condition in the following flowery yet energetic terms: "It is my unpleasant task, in placing the exact condition of

---

5.—History demands the truth regardless of *De mortuis nil nisi bonum;* a study of our Widow and Orphan Endowment cannot forbear to disclose the grave errors which prevented the adoption of a sound system. Grand Secretary Ullman is gone from this world to that realm where our errors are forgiven, especially if these were of the head and not of the heart.

the District before you to state frankly and un-
reservedly, that manifestations of disapproval
have been loud and numerous, to the extent of
engendering such feelings of hostility among the
members, as to create an antagonism directly
prejudicial and perilous to our success and welfare. It follows then, as a matter of course, that
we are at a standstill, and our influential position
in the Order on account of this internal dissension is seriously threatened. By patiently investigating into the cause for this condition of
things, the solution at once becomes patent. *An
increased mortality over previous years*, centennial
statue, mileage and intellectual assessments, have
imposed somewhat larger payments on the individual member, and thus awakened the apparent
dissatisfaction existing."

And the message closes with the remark that
" The District ship is sailing in troubled waters,
and the waves, fomented by dissension, sweep
over her with resistless force, quivering under the
repeated attacks of the rushing waters of selfishness, as they pour a deluge over the deck
with fiendish delight, and gloat over the puny
efforts of a crew, disorganized and disunited,
amidst strife and discord, while destruction seems

swift and certain. The danger increases, for a great storm of mistrust and want of confidence arises, and from all points of the compass comes the furious gale, straining every timber of our noble ship, and so, tossed about from wave to wave, a long line of breakers appears, relentlessly waiting to crush and annihilate her."

To stem this torrent of dissension, the requisite number of representatives requested (in July, 1879), that a special meeting of the G. L. be called for certain purposes, naming : FIRSTLY—to consider the stability of the Endowment Fund, i. e., to ascertain whether the same can be further maintained and what steps are necessary to be taken for that purpose."

In accordance with that application, a special meeting of D G. L. No, 1 was convened on Oct 12th, 1879 for the purpose of considering the subject therein mentioned, foremost among them "the stability of the Endowment fund."

The President had " collated the statistical facts connected therewith, so that by the light of the experience in the past, we can safely estimate our need of the present and provide for the wants and security of the future."

How slightly he understood the subject is

shown by his remarks thereon saying: " We learn
from these facts that the death rate of the District for ten years was $7 \, 5/_{10}$ per cent, or an average of about $\frac{3}{4}$ of 1 per cent for each year, and
the average rate for that period on each death,
18 cents; that 514 deaths occurred with a cost to
each member of $87 92, averaging nearly $8 80
annually, besides accumulating a "Surplus Fund'
of $55,000. And it has been ascertained that
the average age of the membership when the endowment system went into effect, remains in
about the same ratio to-day. The best sources
of information place this record as the maintained
average of deaths in every decade, provided, of
course, that there is an infusion of new life by the
accession of members, which aid materially in the
average of ages, except only in case of general
disaster and epidemic; as a guarantee for this
the protection of the " Reserve fund " must be
invoked, and it is substantially claimed by the
same authority that the limit of the payment from
same authority that the limit of the payment
from this fund over the one per cent. Death
Rate—with its accumulating surplus and interest—will maintain itself for each decade."

Had he understood the question he would

have said : " We learn from these facts that
for ten years (from 1869-1879), the annual
death rate of the District — being from 6
to 9 out of every 1000 members—increased but
little, and has not yet reached one per cent.; but
this is attributable to the very large accession of
young men, doubling the number of our membership in these ten years. So large an increase
cannot be expected to continue, and even if it
were to continue can but *retard* the inevitable
advance of average age, not prevent the mortality from increasing so as to soon exceed one per
cent. The average rate on each death for that
period was 18 cents; had we maintained this rate,
at least, instead of reducing it to 14 cents, we
might from 1874-1879 have accumulated a Reserve fund of just *three* times its present
amount, and by retaining this rate until we exceeded ten thousand members, might gradually
have obtained an adequate reserve fund. As
514 deaths occurred, imposing a cost of $87.92
to each member, it can be easily calculated that
the 514 deceased members paid only $45,000
into the fund, while their families received from
it $514,000, and as this loss must increase from
year to year, even if the rate of mortality were

to remain at about the same ratio, it must end in failure."

The best sources of information[1] tell us "that societies whose members are simply required to meet the current risk of the year, are undoubtedly the most objectionable of all sorts of benefit societies. They do not recognize the principle which is the foundation of all true friendly societies : that of making a provision in youth for the winter of life, and it may be easily shown that if an attempt be made to evade it, the formation of a friendly society is impossible."

It is, however, substantially claimed by the same authority "That this vital defect should be, and can be, easily remedied by basing the insurance upon such ratable assessments as will not only cover its cost now, but also provide for the cost of the same at an advanced age, placing it, in fact, upon a sound mathematical basis, which is susceptible of clear demonstration. This will secure a confidence in, and permanency of the association, which cannot otherwise be had."

Thus would the President have addressed the

1.—Professor Neilson, the highest English authority on Friendly Societies.

members of that special convention of District
Grand Lodge No. 1, had he understood the subject, thus would he have said, had he not disregarded the recommendations of our executive
committee, which, in its official report for 1878
published my Treatise on Fraternal Endowments
with a view to set forth the defects and point
out the remedies, a work which received the
commendation of the best insurance authorities,
and which materially contributed to the improvement of the plans of other mutual benefit associ-
tions. But that very eloquent president preferred
to study fine phrases rather than dry facts and
figures, or the report of our Constitution Grand
Lodge which adopted the recommendation to
our Districts, " to improve their endowment laws
by wise legislation, and to apply every information available, in order to make these laws permanently successful, so as to keep faith with the
promises and expectations held out to their
members."

Instead of recommending any improvement, he
arrived at the following peroration : " Let the
judgment go forth to-day from you whether we
shall reiterate the declaration of our principles,
as laid down, in the preamble of our Order—or

whether we shall inaugurate a new policy, and declare, now and for all time, that the ambitions and aims of District No. 1 were, and are only, the formation of a Life Insurance Company."

As if a "Life Insurance Company" were a reproach. Yes, a Life Insurance Company that makes promises which cannot be fulfilled, one that professes to give insurance for less than half-cost, one that robs Peter to pay Paul, one that mismanages or misapplies the funds of its members—is a fraud and a disgrace ; but purely mutual life assurance, based on correct principles, honestly, prudently and economically managed, is one of the noblest devices of human wisdom, one of the greatest achievements of association and co-operation, of which modern civilization may well be proud. *Fraternal Life Insurance* based on the same scientific principles, the same well-established laws of mortality, but pruned of the defects and excrescences of *life insurance for profit*, and established for no other purpose than to provide for our widows and orphans, for those we love and who are dependent on our support— to provide for these after our death—"is the realization of fraternity without the destruction of independence and individuality; it is a charity

without cant, which enriches the giver and does
not humiliate the receiver." [2]

It must be stated, however, that the error of
the President was one of the head and not of the
heart, his honesty of purpose and indefatigable
zeal in furthering the principles and aims of
our brotherhood are thankfully acknowledged
and of record in the annals of the Order.

After the reading of his message, a printed
copy of which was handed to every representative (160 were present), the signers to the petition on behalf of Manhattan Lodge, No. 156,
explained the reasons for the call of this special
session and stated, that the "Endowment" question in the District was one of the principal
causes of this action, and that measures should
be taken to insure its safety in the future.

Resolutions were offered; one, that the rate
of assessment should not be less than 16 cents
for each death; another that the rate of Endowment remain 13 cents for next year and that the
"general" fund, (collected during twenty-five
years for the purpose of giving our aged and

2.—Elizur Wright, Savings Bank Life Insurance, Boston,
1872, folio edition, page 17.

helpless brethren a " Home "), should hence-
forth be known as the reserve fund!

Finally, after a long discussion, the following
motion was adopted :

Resolved, That a committee of fifteen be appointed,
to whom shall be referred the resolutions of Manhattan Lodge, 3 and the amendment of Bro. J. E. New-

---

3.—Washington Lodge, No. 19, also recommended, in a
masterly written memorial, that the "death rate" be increased from 13 to 15 cents per member. But no mention
is made of it in the official proceedings ! It contained the
following unpleasant but truthful words :

" It cannot be denied that the representatives have, at all
the annual meetings of the Grand Lodge, *repeated the error*,
(in spite of all warnings of the several General Committees)
of reducing the 'death-rate,' thereby making the formation
of a proper reserve-fund an impossibility.

' Consequently it is our sacred duty to change this state
of affairs and increase the 'death-rate' from 13 to 15 cents
per member, *instead of stretching out our hands for money
not collected, nor lawfully applicable, for this purpose*.

" By the adoption of such a measure the Endowment Reserve Fund would represent a capital of about $200,000
within five years, i.e., in 1885, and if continued would
amount (with interest and compound interest) to $650,000
in 1890, as everybody can easily calculate. Properly managed, this capital would of course increase proportionately
in the future.

"According to the opinion of experts, these amounts
would suffice to insure forever the payment of $1000 to the
heirs of every brother, and would place the further existence of this beneficial provision beyond all doubt.

" The number of deaths for the year 1879 will probably

burger(to amalgamate the general and endowment fund
funds), also that the lodges and representatives be in-
vited to send in their plans and views up to the 15th
of November to that committee, who shall engage an
actuary, and be ready with a full and comprehensive
report and plan for action at the next session of this
Grand Lodge.

On January 25th, 1880, District Grand Lodge,
No. 1 assembled in the city of New York, and
the Committee on Endowment, appointed at the
preceding special session (Oct. 12th, 1879), presented *three* reports :

FIRST: The majority of said committee was
of the opinion that "as long as the membership
can be maintained at the present average age,
and the payments continue as heretofore, the
stability of the fund is established; . . . .
that the average age of the members has not
changed materially during the past ten years,

--- —

not exceed 80, but let us say it were 90, (i. e., 1 per cent of
the 9000 members of our District). Each brother would
then, at the rate of 15 cents, have to pay the (enormous ! !)
amount of $13.50 per annum. or *scarcely more than half the
sum which any good Insurance Company would charge as
annual premium for men averaging 35 years of age.*

"Now, we ask where is the reason for all the noise and
commotion which for months has been called forth by some
lodges and which found its echo in the public Press?

"*We* cannot see it."

while *in the future it will decrease* considerable, as the new element which is constantly being added consists chiefly of young men; . . and if in any one year the burden should be greater than of other years, our brethren will not hesitate to pay the additional assessment; . . . . that as long as the present average age of our members remains as it is, the death rate will not be more than from ¾ to 1 per cent. . . . . That an expert actuary of well known ability corroborates the statement above made . . . and, considering all these facts, it would not be necessary to change the rate of assessment; . . . . but we may with propriety try some new method, by which future success may be more firmly established . . . . and therefore recommend that hereafter an annual assessment of $13 per member be levied. By the adoption of such a measure, the Endowment Reserve fund would in a few years represent a capital, such as would remove every doubt concerning the solvency of the Endowment and make the same more secure than any insurance company . . . No part of the Reserve fund shall be used for the payment of any endowment, excepting in case the death rate in any one year shall exceed 1¼ per cent.

of the membership." . . . and "if the re-commendations of this committee are adopted, the stability and future maintenance of the Endowment is forever secured."

Thus ran the long and anxiously expected report of the majority (nine members) of the committee; and its minority (of five members) heartily concurred in the sentiments expressed in the majority-report *as to the security of the Endowments*, but recommended a scheme whereby the funds were to be held by the lodges invested in the U. S. bonds, and the assessment rate was to remain 13 cents.

The unanimity with which fourteen out of fifteen members of a committee, consisting of Past Presidents, distinguished brothers of the Order, men of a high degree of ability and intelligence; agreed and subscribed to such palpable fallacies, is one of the phenomena of popular delusions. But the statement of that committee, that they "deemed it advisable to consult an expert actuary of well known ability, who, after careful study of all points, corroborated the statements made above" is more than a mistake. No actuary of any ability could

ever admit such *absurdities.*[4] Either the committee must have been deceived by an expert in

— ---

4.—"Absurdities" is a strong, harsh expression ; but the
members of that committee, many of whom I know and
highly respect, will admit, after kindly studying the follow
ing, that it is fully justified :

Supposing it were true or possible, as stated and corroborated by their actuary, that the average age could remain the
same, and that thus the death rate in any decade would not
be more than from ¾ to 1 per cent; then (taking the membership to continue at 9000, as the Committee itself did
the highest death rate would be 90, or in fifty years 4500,
deaths. Now, assuming that all these deaths would occur
among the original members only, and that none of the
additional members joining during these 50 years, were to
die (another impossibility) even then, at the end of the 50th
year, there would still remain living 4500 of the original
members, whose age could not be less than between 75 and
90 years! And under the above assumption of 90 deaths
per annum another half century would have to pass away
before these remaining 4500 very old members could depart
from life !

The expert in wondrous cheap insurance may tell you :
The lapses must be taken into consideration." Well, do
so: assume that 1500 members have withdrawn and it
would still leave 3000 instead of 4500 members who—being
after 50 years near four-score years of age—cannot be
expected to live much longer, while according to the absurd
assumption of a permanent death rate not exceeding 90 pe

those fraudulent schemes,—the Superintendent of Insurance of New York, the Hon. John A. McCall, Jr., said of them in his last report: "The pretences and promises of the managers of some of these schemes would be grotesque, if they were not put forth in a serious way,—or they have been imposed upon by a wag, wishing some sport at their expense. Who the Committee's actuary "of well known ability" was, is nowhere told; but the accounts of that year's expenses divulge the fact that the enormous sum of $20 was paid as "actuary's fee for Endowment committee."

The committee could certainly not get an Elizur Wright, or a Sheppard Homans, or any other respectable actuary "of well known ability"

———··——

year, they would have to reach an age which, under the divine laws of human life and death, is not granted to *one* man out of thousands.

Experts of fraudulent insurance schemes assume that 9 per cent of the members would annually lapse (or be dropped) while 1 per cent would die; and that in the same proportion new, young members could annually be induced to join, so that after ten years none of the original members are left! Thus, and thus only, can the statement be corroborated that "the rate in any decade will not be more than from ¾ to 1 per cent.

to study all points of our Endowment system and give an opinion for $20. But the committee might have saved even those $20; its members needed only to consult the report of the Executive Committee for 1877–1878, wherein it is shown and proven by plain calculations, easily understood by any one who can figure, that no probable addition of new and younger members could prevent the advance of age and, consequently, the increasing mortality in any society.

One member of that committee, however, (Bro. Isidor Metzger) had evidently well informed himself, had carefully considered the subject, and being satisfied that his conclusions were correct, had the manhood to express them in a

MINORITY-REPORT OF ONE.

This report deserves a careful study, the more so, as it may well serve for the basis of the first correct solution of this yet unsolved problem in District No. 1.

He introduces his report with the modest remark that : at first sight it may appear both plausible and proper to presume, that the views of so large a majority must be correct, and the opinions of one, in the minority, false and illogical; but he hopes that an unbiased judgment may yet find some few grains of truth in the assertions of the latter, particularly as the latter has this much in his favor : that while the majority offer results without stating their reasons, the minority gives reasons for arriving at his conclusions.

First, however, before stating his reasons, he asks: "Does it require any argument to prove that a man of 55 should pay almost double of what a man of 35 has to pay to have his life insured ? Are the prospects of life of a man of the age of 55 the same as those of a man of 35, assuming, of course to be both equally in good health ? . . . Is it therefore not self evident that the method so far pursued in the endowment matter is erroneous and contrary to every known law either of mortality or insurance ?" No answer to this question is given in his report, nor anywhere in the records of the various Grand Lodges; and yet this question is a most important one.

From the standpoint of theory, on the mathematically correct basis of life insurance business, —assessments as well as premiums would have to be equitably graded according to age. But, aside from the fact that the Court of Appeals of the Order B'nai B'rith has decided[5] in favor of *uniformity* of taxation, and has declared the grading of rates unconstitutional, sound and weighty arguments, based on the higher stand-point of fraternal benevolence, speak strongly in favor of a uniform rate of assessment; and it can be shown and demonstrated by figures that *within certain limitations* this method is safely admissible: Aye, taking the adjustments by which its defects may be neutralized into account, a uniform rate is *preferable* for a fraternal benevolent institution. The equality of contributions and of benefits at once distinguishes the truly benevolent institution from the mere insurance business, and entitles FRATERNAL endowment societies to the motto, "Alter alterius Onera Portate."

The NECESSARY LIMITATIONS are, that none be admitted to membership, (as far as the endowment is concerned), above the age of 45, none who are sick or subject to herditary disease, and that none but the widow and orphans or *designated* members of the family, or purely

---

5.—Appeal X, Hellbron et al, vs. D. G. L. No. 2. Report of the Executive Committee of C. G. L , 1872-73.

benevolent institutions, be allowed to receive the benefit. The PRINCIPAL ADJUSTMENTS are the great saving in expenses, the easy and perfect control of the management, the exclusion of any feature of profit; and the fact that all lapses enure to the benefit of the faithful adherents of the Order. These limitations and adjustments reduce the actual cost of insurance by more than the difference in mortality between the ages of 25 and 45 years, which difference is not over $3. per $1000 annually.

Practically, age alone is not a perfectly reliable guide, and uniform rates for men of the same age are not always equitably just. From the uncertainty of individual life nobody can predict his own term; hence it cannot be called unfair,—else it would be just as unfair that a young member, who dies after paying but few years a low rate, receive the same benefit as an old member, who attains the age of 75 or more years, and pays a high rate. Moreover, there are two methods of grading mortality rates; one with rates which do not increase with age after entry, and another with rates which increase after age of entry. Both have, practically, some serious defects: If the rates are graded according to age and do *not* increase with advancing age after entry, it must result, before long, in unequal taxation on members of the same age, but admitted at different ages,—thereby creating dissatisfaction ; and the rates must be loaded so as to accumulate a reserve fund, no less in the aggregate amount than under a uniform rate, but more complicated. If the rates increase after age of entry, they would be low at first, as no large reserve fund is required under this method, but they advance with the increasing mortality after the "turn of life," from age 60, so as to become oppressive, practically FORCING old members to withdraw, losing the benefit intended for their widows and orphans.

THE FOLLOWING TABLE may serve to compare those methods. The figures (columns 1, 2 and 7) show the number of members of District No. 1, I. O. B. B., at their respective ages on Jan. 1, 1885 (ascertained from official reports of its Lodges).

1	2	3	4	5	6	7	8	9	10	11	12	
Ages, From...... to....	No. of Members at the respective ages.	Per cent. of mortality.	No. of deaths ac. to exp. mor'ty.	Annual as'ments incr. with age.	Amount realized from these Assessments at the respect. ages.	No. of Members from 21-50, others grouped as before.	Annual Assess-ments not in-	creasing up to age of 50, and am't realized fr. such assessm'ts.	Uniform rate not increasing.	Amount realized therefrom.	Amounts contributed from age 21-7½ by each Member.	
											At increasing rates.	At unif'm non-inc's'g rates.
21—30	1000	0.8	8	$ 8	$ 8,000	⎫ 6830	$ 15	$ 102,450	$ 18	$ 122,940	$ 72	$ 162
31—40	2960	0.9	26	9	26,640	⎬					90	180
41—45	1490	1.0	15	10	14,900						50	90
46—50	1380	1.2	16	12	16,560	⎭ 1064	18	19,152	18	19,152	60	90
51—55	1064	1.7	18	17	18,088	757	24	18,168	18	13,626	85	90
56—60	757	2.4	18	24	18,168	330	34	11,220	18	5,940	120	90
61—65	330	3.4	11	34	11,220	157	50	7,850	18	2,826	170	90
66—70	157	5.0	8	50	7,850	105	80	8,400	18	1,890	250	90
71—75	105	8.0	8	80	8,400						400	90
Totals,	9243	—	128	—	$129,826	9243	—	$167,240	—	$166,374	1297	972

A careful study of these figures will convey more information to thoughtful readers than many pages of arguments could give.

Having considered the question left unanswered in the minority report, and shown that the METHOD pursued in our Endowment system is *not* as defective nor as erroneous as it appears, if judged from the standpoint of theory; that, on the contrary, as a practical method, properly adjusted and based on a SUFFICIENT uniform contribution, it is preferable for fraternal organizations ; let us now return to that interesting report of *one* (Jan., 1880). It proceeds thus : " The absolute falsity of the proposition *that the average age of the members will* DECREASE CONSIDERABLY *in years to come owing to the addition of a new and presumably younger element into the Order*, is demonstrated by the following example : Assuming our membership in District No. 1 to be 9,000 at an average age of 40, it is evident that next year the average age will be 41; or, in other words, the entire body will be collectively 9,000 years older. To keep the average age at that figure (not to reduce it, as asserted above) it would require an influx of not less than 900 members whose average age must not exceed 30 years; and each succeeding year, instead of alleviating the evil, would only

heighten it.—Statistics show that our gain in membership does not and never will keep pace with what
is required to maintain the average age."[6]

6.—The following table, showing the increase in membership and mortality, in District No. 1, from the Statistical
Reports of its G. L. for the years 1874 to 1885 furnishes
mathematical proof that the average age must have increased also, notwithstanding the large addition of a new and
young element. This calculation assumes the average age
of the members in 1874 at 40, (it was then 40.66 in District
No. 2,); the average age of all deceased members at 50, and
that of the new additional members at 30 years only; and
yet, under these most favorable assumptions, their present
average age must be 45 years.

Year	Date. Jan. 1.	Membership	Average Age.	Deaths.	Per cent. Mortality.	Addition of New M'bers.	Increase in Membership.	Increase in Percentage.
1	1874	6568	40.00	39	0.6	343	304	4.6
2	1875	6872	40.40	58	0.9	508	450	6.5
3	1876	7322	40.53	55	0.8	317	262	3.6
4	1877	7584	41.00	52	0.7	570	518	6.8
5	1878	8102	41.10	77	0.9	470	393	4.8
6	1879	8495	41.39	89	1.0	317	228	2 7
7	1880	8723	41.72	85	1 0	162	77	0.9
8	1881	8800	42.42	90	1.0	236	146	1.7
9	1882	8946	43.00	85	0.9	250	165	1.8
10	1883	9111	43.54	106	1.2	247	141	1.5
11	1884	9252	44.09	100	1.1	91	dec. 9	0.0
12	1885	9243	44.86	—	—	—	—	—

"The assertion that as long as we keep our average age at 40, the rate of mortality will not exceed 1 per cent. is not combatted; but having demonstrated that it is physically impossible to keep our average age so low, it very naturally follows that our mortality must yearly increase....and if we desire to perpetuate the 'Endowment Fund,' we must make provision for that contingency, so that all may equally receive the benefit of the same, whether we be cut down in the prime of life or may reach the age of three score and ten. We cannot continue as we have done; we cannot assume to pay out to the heirs of our members more than we receive, without drifting into bankruptcy. How is the deficiency to be supplied? It is very simple to say, from the future accession of new members; but that method will come to a speedy end, as the history of institutions based on this principle will show....In conclusion, if the statement made, that our death rate will never exceed 1 per cent. be true, it would require just 100 years before the last member (even if we did not get another member,) would have died."7

7.—The statement that, (did we not get another member) it would require 100 years before the last of 9000 members would die, should our death rate never exceed 1 per cent—is

The said minority report further expresses it as his opinion that: "We must either be prepared, as the increase in mortality comes, to pay the onerous increasing tax required, or we must make now some provision for the future."

In further explanation the report quotes from the author of this Study, and arrives at the following re-

---

a fair illustration of the gross mistakes which even very intelligent men may commit in calculating the simplest problem of life insurance.

As 1 per cent of 9000=90, and as 100x90=9000, this statement, at first sight, appears correct; but as the number surviving is annually reduced by 1 per cent, the number of deaths is also proportionately reduced, so that after 100 years over 3000 members would remain living, and after 220 years 1000 members would not yet have died! At this rate it would take a century for the last one hundred men, and this at a death rate annually increasing in percentage from 1 per cent in the first to 50 per cent in the 99th year. In like manner the 90 deaths annually, as assumed in above statement, would NOT be a death rate of 1 per cent, excepting in the first year; in the 51st year, when but half the members, (4500) wouldbe left, this number of deaths would already be 2 per cent, and in the 99th year it would be 50 per cent of the remaining 180 members. While this error is of no practical moment, as nobody is expected to reach Methuselah's age, it shows how easily fallacies are taken for truths.

sult: "'The amount annually payable by every member of District No. 1, should be not less than $18, and anything less than that sum would result in providing for only a part and not for all of the members of the District."...."The issue which instigated this investigation, having been brought about by a large number of brethren who find the increasing taxes too onerous to bear—no remedy like the above can be expected to be adopted; the only alternative that the undersigned can therefore recommend, would be the reduction of the Endowment from $1,000 to $500 ; and an annual assessment of $9.00 per annum, payable quarterly, in advance, and invested under the direction of the Grand Lodge, or any committee, in such a manner as to bear not less than 5 per cent. interest per annum; and while the first decade, under an average mortality, would show a large surplus, subsequent years, with an increased death rate would show that our resources were but just sufficient to meet the legitimate demand made upon us....I question whether the above proposition will meet with your approval; but, if I have only succeeded in convincing a handful of your worthy body of the correctness of my theory, I feel well repaid....and will leave to 'Time, Patience and Perseverence,' which conquer all things, the ultimate adoption, perhaps in some modified form, of my views."

The doubts of the said report of one, as to whether the proposition contained therein would meet with approval, were but too well founded.

Our representatives probably thought "'Twere to consider too curiously," to consider so odd a proposition. After a few hours' debate, rich in words and poor in arguments, the *"previous question"* was ordered, and the following motion was adopted :

"That inasmuch as it is not advisable at present to increase the taxation of the lodges, and that as the endowment law has worked successfully up to the the present, the same be continued for another year, and the three reports as submitted be laid on the table."

A motion to increase the per capita tax for endowments from 13 to 15 cents, and an amendment to make it 14 cents,—were both defeated.

Were the members who signed the majority report allowed to reconsider their action to-day, most of them would sign and vote for that minority report of one ; aye, they themselves would now scarcely believe that they signed as they did, were the record thereof not preserved in print.

This is no reproach; it shows a growth in wisdom. Fools only do not admit that they have erred and are ashamed to learn. Thus, the Endowment remained as it was—unchanged.

Whether the brethren of District No. 1 were willing to adopt the views of the majority, or, as good American citizens, had agreed to abide by the legal decision of the majority — right or wrong,—certain it is, that "the storm subsided," peace and harmony were, for a time, restored.

In January, 1881, the President's Message referred to the Endowment in the following words: "Our death-rate during the past year has been about the same as that of the year previous, one death less being reported than heretofore ; it is therefore gratifying to perceive that although our average is constantly advancing in age, we are equally fortunate in maintaining our equilibrium; *the per capita dues therefore can be safely(?) retained at the present rate for the coming year.*"

The committee on Widows and Orphans Reserve Fund of District No. 1, also reported : "We find that the present dues of 13 cents leave a fair surplus, being at the same time not burdensome upon our members and, by degrees, augmenting our Reserve Fund to safe proportions, we recommend that the same remain for the next year as the pro rata rate."

As early as January, 1882, however, the President mentioned, in his message, that the Endowment Laws caused animated discussion among our constituents, and urged the importance of a small increase in the per capita dues, in order that this prominent and interesting feature (the Endowment) might be perpetuated. He further suggested " that a special committee be appointed, to report, a year hence, their findings as to our future wants in this direction, based upon unbiassed opinions, and with ample time for reflection, such as is not granted us when in convention assembled."

The committee on that President's Message justly praised this document as one of vast research and lucid reasoning, and reported : " In respect to the Endowment, we do not deem it expedient at present to increase the per capita assessment, but heartily concur with our brother president, and perceive the necessity of the appointment of a committee as suggested by him, to secure the stability of our Endowment and our future wants in that direction."

This recommendation was adopted and the committee appointed.

———

Another year had elapsed, another year added to the age of our members. The Grand Lodge had re-assembled ; and on this occasion the special committee on Endowment presented a unanimous report. The president in his message to that convention, on January 28th, 1883, referred to this special committee as "composed of brethren of experience and judgment, who had doubtless digested, and would present, a plan worthy of proper consideration.[1]

The report correctly represents the views generally entertained respecting the Endowment Fund, and expresses the hope that "the most cursory review of the statistics presented will demonstrate to the least expert mathematician, that a grievous error has been committed by those who were the sponsors for the present

———

1.—The great length of this Report, filling over nine pages of the printed proceedings, and the fact that it was afterwards printed for distribution among all the members of the District, will necessitate merely a short synopsis of the same.

plan.......Any ordinary arithmetician could have shown readily and clearly what number of young men would be necessary to be added annually to justify the calculation based on a stationary average age or on retarding its advance to such a degree that it would hardly be fractional." The report defines the position of this fund, in its relation to those who contribute towards it, thus: " There are members who scout the idea of likening the Endowment Fund to an insurance. They set forth that the Order B'nai B'rith existed before the endowment feature was introduced ; that the fund is simply one of the benevolent objects of the institution, and should not be based on those mathematical principles which obtain in ordinary life insurance ; for, say they, so long as the members are willing to pay the assessments levied upon them to this fund, so long will it exist as one of the benevolent features of the District. This aspect of the case would certainly be reasonable, if the endow ment laws were based upon the principle that 'we pay as long as we can, (*or are willing to pay!*) and no longer.'...... As the laws are framed at present, however, the District guarantees to the heirs of members, who have com-

plied with the provisions of the law, at their
death, the payment of $1000,......thus assum-
ing a debt which it is in honor bound to pay.
......Let us, then, see whether we can fulfill
the expectations of our members, if the present
plan is continued."

The report then invites the attention of the
members to some statistics, which it presents in
their simplest form ;[2] showing first, the increase
in membership from 1870 to 1882. Here it may
readily be seen that there is but little hope of
retarding in any appreciative degree the steady
advance of the average age of members. Then
the statistics of the deaths of the same years are

2.—The Committee says: "that the great difficulty has
ever been that in demonstrating problems of this nature,
recourse to figures is absolutely necessary; usually, however, the array is so great, that the ordinary mind stands
aghast and fails to understand them. Many timely reforms,
even in this Grand Lodge, have been wrecked by a display
of this character." But while a display of figures is useless and sometimes worse than useless in *debate*, it is no
less indispensable to a thorough examination of such problems. Those who wish to study the subject must be able
to examine the figures, and those who cannot study these
should be guided by trustworthy men who are able and
willing to do so.

given, and a computation with these figures shows, that while the increase of membership from 1870 to 1882 was 94 per cent., the increase of deaths during the same period was 164 per cent.[3]

3.—In the last decade, from 1874 to 1884, the increase in membership (from 6568 to 9252 members) was only 40 per cent., while the increase in the death-rate was over 170 per per cent. (from 39 deaths in 1874 to 106 deaths in 1884), reaching a mortality which, according to Am. Experience tables, would indicate the age of 47 years, while the *average age* was only 44 years. "Average Age" furnishes no correct basis for accurately calculating the probable mortality. For instance: 100 members aged 30 each, and 100 members aged 60 each, having together a total age of 9000 years, are said to have an average of age of 45; but while we find from the Table of Mortality that out of 200 men at the age of 45, (death rate 11 in 1000) 2.2 would die in one year, we find from the same reliable table that

Out of 100 aged 30, the death-rate is 0.85
" 100 " 60, " 2.67
—— Total, 3.52

Consequently out of these 200 members, having an average age of 45 years, the death-rate would be at least *three*, and not only *two* members.

This may sufficiently explain why the "*Average Age*" furnishes *no accurately correct* basis for calculations of mortality; practically, however, not even the most accurate calculation could be relied upon for a small number of mem-

"This exhibit must assuredly demolish the assumption so long and so unwarrantedly maintained, that the "average age" of the members will always remain the same, and that no fear need be entertained from that source."

"Having shown that our age is steadily advancing, and, as a natural consequence, the number of deaths—increasing," the committee had "no hesitation in saying that unless speedy measures were adopted, and of such a nature as would prove a remedy for the loss of the past ......failure would be inevitable.

Earnestly and eloquently the report appeals to the Grand Lodge; to look this question seriously in the face; to consider it as men and brethren seeking each other's good; to take wise counsel; there being yet time to effect a remedy. It alludes to former attempts; but "No sooner does

---

bers; and in a society where no persons above the age of 45 years are admitted, the average age furnishes an approximately correct and very convenient basis for calculation. Thus, in the 9243 members of District No. 1, at their present *average age* (45 years), the probable mortality would this year (1885) be, according to the Am. Experience Mortality Table: 104 deaths; according to the Actuaries' Combined Experience Table, 111 deaths; calculated *separately for each age*, the result would be: 128 deaths. (See page 115.)

the question arise than a sort of demagogical spirit springs up in its discussion—an opposition based on utter ignorance of the interests involved—a kind of catering to and currying of favor with the masses, takes the place of reason and duty, and thus legislation upon this question has ever resulted in the adoption of measures which were (*seemed*) expedient, instead of those which are just. The time has now arrived when such methods must be swept aside. Action, looking to the perpetuity of the Fund, must be taken immediately ; delay will prove disastrous."

The report offers further excellent arguments; also figures based on the average expectancy of life, (which for a healthy man of 41 is 27 years,) showing that at 5 per cent. interest an annual payment of $17.42 will in 27 years produce $1000;[4] and after due consideration and calculation the committee says : "that 18 cents *per capita* for each death will yield the annual contribution as shown above, and create a reserve

---

4.—The committee overlooked, or else purposely ignored, the fact that out of the annual payments of the surviving members, the endowments of those who died from year to year had to be paid, leaving only a part of the members' contributions to accumulate at interest.

fund of adequate proportions."

After some additional, highly valuable suggestions as to the admission of members, and other necessary safeguards, the committee report closes with the following words : "we would ask you to study the questions herein discussed, to the end that the reforms advocated may be adopted, so that the system will be a real blessing, and secure for itself and our beloved institution enduring prosperity."

Did the representatives study the question? Did they mind the earnest appeal for the speedy . adoption of measures to remedy the loss of the past? Did they listen to the wise counsel of their own committee, "brethren of experience and judgment," as the President had designated them, and as every member of the Grand Lodge had to admit them to be? Did this Grand Lodge take any action looking to the perpetuity of the fund?

Alas! far from it. The demagogical motion : "that the report be printed for distribution, that copies be sent to all the members of the District through the-respective lodges, and that the consideration of the report be deferred to the next annual session of the Grand Lodge," was adopted.

The opposition, so well characterized in said
report, defeated every motion that the rate of
assessment for the coming year be made 15,
or even 14 cents; and the motion that it remain
at 13 cents was adopted. Thus another year
was lost !

The said able, elaborate and unanimous report
of the committee had been printed and faithfully
distributed to the various lodges of District No.
1, by its indefatigable secretary; copies were
freely sent to the members by their respective
lodges; and the eminent chairman of that committee expressed the hope that "as our representatives are mostly business men, possessed of
sound, practical common sense, who from their
daily walks of life knew better than any other
class of men that *figures can not lie*, he had no
reason to fear the final result.   On the contrary,
he was very hopeful that this 'bone of contention' would soon be disposed of, so far as District No. 1 was concerned, in a manner as rational as it would be satisfactory." (*Reports of the
members of the Executive Committee, 1882–1883,
page 10*)

Vain hope ! Men may be very good business
men, may be of sound, practical common sense,

and yet understand nothing about Life Insurance.[12] The majority of business men have neither time nor inclination to study such reports,

---

12. The *Boston Globe* has just published a pamphlet containing "Opinions of Eminent Men of the Country" on LIFE
INSURANCE, letters and interviews, from which the following quotations are in point :

" I have not made much of a study of Life Insurance."
—Senator Henry M. Teller, (who was Secretary of the In-
terior under President Arthur.

"I know very little about Life Insurance."—Postmaster
Pearson.

"I have not paid much attention to Life Insurance.—
Mayor Grace.

"I don't know anything about it."—W. H. Vanderbilt.

"I have not considered the matter carefully."— David
Dudley Field.

"Like many other business men, I have never had time
to thoroughly examine an institution in which I have confidence, and in which I carry several policies—C. A. Lori-
mer, Chicago.

" I do not know that I given sufficient attention to
the subject of Life Insurance to qualify me to give an
opinion that would be worth anything"—E. H. Capen,
President Taft's College.

" If I had any wisdom on the life insurance question, you
should certainly have it."—Rev. M. J. Savage of Boston.

"Life Insurance is a subject which has never received
very careful attention from me."—Bishop Wingfield of Cal.

"Upon this subject I really have no knowledge whatever, though insured for $21,000."—P. B. Plumb, U. S.
Senator of Kansas.

much less the figures of mortality tables and their calculations ; they can not easily comprehend how a tax which is all-sufficient for present wants, and besides that, yields an annual surplus, gradually increasing to several hundred thousand dollars, should need still more of an increase.

The committee hoped to convince the representatives of the justice of its proposition by showing that in any sound Life Insurance Company a man of the average age of our members would have to pay a much greater tax. But other fraternal organizations and assessment in-

---

"I have not given the matter of Life Insurance that attention."—E. A. Perry, Governor of Florida.

"I have not given sufficient study to Life Insurance."—Gen. Slocum of New York.

"I am in no sense an expert in the matter of Life Insurance."—G. D. Morgan of New York.

"I am too busy to go deeply into the subject of Life Insurance just now."—A. B. Farcuhar of Penn.

"I insured because.....all classes of successful men insure. Many of these men know much more than I do. I am glad to take their advice."—E. R. Wheelock of N. Y.

"I have not sufficient knowledge, etc."—Senator Gibson of La.

'I have never made any careful study of the subject."—Dorman B. Eaton, Comm. U. S. Civil Service.

But they all recognize its benefits and—insure.

surance societies, offer larger benefits at lower rates and charge the old system of life insurance as faulty in the extreme. Which is right? Even with those brethren who fully recognize that the tax of 13 cents is insufficient and who gave the subject earnest thought, the proper amount to be paid is mere guesswork; some propose 18 cents, others 16 cents, still others would be satisfied with 15 cents. Which amount is correct? which is wrong? For it would be just as wrong to ex-act too much as not enough.

In matters of mathematical science, common sense alone cannot be relied upon; guesswork will not inspire confidence. But "why not adopt a system based upon scientific calculation *and fitted to our peculiar* condition by competent minds? Such a one is in successful operation in District No. 2, and under the circumstances I deem best that it be incorporated in the laws of all other Districts." This was the advice of Bro. *Julius Bien*, whose wonderfully clear head, broad and deep erudition, coupled with the most unselfish devotion to the Order, entitle him, beyond dispute, to be its chief and monitor. Unfortunately, his words are not read by the majority and are remembered by but few; unfortunately, 'most every representative imagines his own mind "so clear in his great office" that it renders him wise enough to decide every question—whether of law, finance, mathematics or any other science ; according to the German adage :

" Wen Gott giebt ein Amt,—giebt er auch Verstand."

Aware of this weakness in many representatives and of the want of any precise scientific demonstration as to the amount required, the President of District No. 1 in his opening Message to the Grand Lodge,—referring to the report of the Special Committee on Endowment, the consideration of which had been deferred to that session; —Jan., 1884, said as follows :

"It is evident that the rate of assessment now being paid is insufficient, and that an increase is absolutely necessary. What the extent of that increase should be, *it is for you to determine*, and, whilst the amount recommended by the special committee may be, for the present, larger than is absolutely necessary, some figure greater than that which we are now paying should be adopted." . . . "If, then, it is your desire that Endowment shall remain a permanent feature of the District, you must make it so by such legislation as will render its continuance absolutely certain. I can see but one alternative, and that is, to eliminate the Endowment entirely from the work of the District, creating either a distinct endowment fund, or leaving it optional with the lodges themselves whether or not they desire to avail themselves of such a benefit."

How little effect these wise words of the President, or the able and elaborate representation of the matter in the Special Committee's report, had on the members or on the Standing Committee on W. and O. fund, is shown by the report of the latter, who recommended, by a vote of four to one, that the endowment tax be increased *one* cent, making it 14 cents, and saying: "that, while not making the burden too heavy, it still will constantly(?) and gradually increase our reserve fund."

"We heartily agree (S. B. Hamburger dissenting,) in the recommendation of the increase in the per capita tax of one cent, making the same 14 cents for the coming year, believing the increase will aid in strengthening the reserve fund, so that in time we will have an endowment fund, the stability of which cannot be questioned."

Had this committee added: *provided* our membership remains or will exceed 9000, and, *provi-*

ded further, that the payment of said tax be collected on the death of every member, not limited
as to the number of deaths which may occur ; in
such case, of course, the stability of the Endowment Fund and the constant increase of its reserve would be beyond question. But as the
committee knew that, according to the Endowment law of District No. 1, the Endowment for
all deaths exceeding one and one-quarter per
cent. of the number of members, was to be paid
out of the reserve fund ; and as by this time it
ought to have known that, with the increasing
age of the members, their mortality would also
increase, the committee might easily have seen
that the STABILITY of which they talked was not
only questionable, but impossible. Without consulting any mortality tables, and by merely looking at the statistics of their own District, they
might have seen that: while in 1874, 39 out of
6568 members died, as early as 1883 106 died
out of 9111 members ; the death rate gradually
increasing, from 6 to 12 out of every 1000 members. Thus, it would be reasonable to assume
that, after another decennium, or perhaps later,
the death rate would increase 2 per cent.; how
would the account then stand ? If the member-

ship increase to 10,000, there would be 200
deaths in one year; amount of Endo ments to
be paid, $200,000 ; 125 deaths, being assessed
for 14 cents from 10,000 members,=$175,000,
weakening the reserve fund by a deficit of $25,-
000. If the membership were to decrease, say
to 8000 members, there would be 160 deaths in
one year, requiring for endowments to be paid
$160,000, while the assessments for 100 deaths
(1¼ per cent.,) at 14 cents would yield scarcely
$112,000, causing a deficit of $48,000.

Hence it required but little foresight and fore-
thought to prognosticate that : far from having
an Endowment Fund the stability of which
could not be questioned, there would, at a time,
not very remote either, be no Endowment Fund
whatever left.

Bro. S. B. H mburger, the chairman of said
committee on the W. and O. committee's report,
accordingly wrote as follows : " I must dissent
from the recommendations of my brethren to increase the ' per capita tax ' one cent, and cannot
agree with their views, that it will strengthen the
reserve fund, that the stability thereof cannot be
questioned. I believe that the endowment system, as it exists at the present time, is wholly

insufficient to secure to the junior members of
our Order, the Endowment which is guaranteed
them by the Constitution. To the end of setting
at rest forever the constant interminable discussion on the subject, I respectfully recommend
that the present Grand Lodge adopt such legislation as will repeal all laws contained in the
District Grand Lodge Laws, affecting the
subject of endowment, and that we recommend
to the Constitution Grand Lodge, the repeal of
the entire Endowment Law, and thus leave the
perplexing question of endowment to the respective Lodges, to be controlled and governed as
they may deem fit and proper."

"Should however this recommendation not
meet your favor, I further recommend, *for the
benefit of those brethren who may depart this life
within the next* TEN *years*, that the "per capita
tax" be increased at least to the sum of sixteen
cents. This amount of increase may seem
exorbitant and burdensome. It will not be if
those of us who are members of three or four
organizations, kindred to our own, will cease to
become members therein, or abolish the endowment."

The discussion of these reports and of the

Endowment questions in general lasted until past midnight of the G. L. Session, January 28th, 1884, and was resumed on the following day; at 4 P. M., as agreed, the vote was taken, first on the motion "to disagree with both reports and to leave the 'per capita tax' at 13 cents." This motion was lost by *one* vote, (48 ayes, 49 nays). Finally the motion to concur in the majority report of the W. and O. Committee, to make the tax 14 cents, was adopted (50 ayes against 48 nays),

Thus the first victory was won, the first little step was taken towards an improvement of the Endowment System in District No. 1, quite insufficient to make it permanently enduring, yet important as the first defeat of the persistent opposition against the least increase, and giving stronger hopes for further improvement in the right direction. Moreover, another amendment was adopted during the last hour of that same session—almost without discussion—which amendment (proposed by the representative of Washington Lodge) is of far greater value than an increase of the tax and by an additional cent would have been, namely: raising the per centage of mortality, for which assessments are to be collected, from one and one quarter to one and one half per cent; so that Endowments in excess of one and one half per cent of the number of members, in any one year, should be paid out of the Reserve-Fund.

By this amendment the Endowment fund would be enduring for at least *20* years!

Far from advocating the said rate and limitation,—as it has serious defects,--it might be desirable, in view of the present agitation in some Lodges, to show by careful arithmancy how this system would work, even were no further improvements to be made and not a single new member added. But a table to this effect, with its many columns of figures, would not be examined by one out of hundreds of our brethren and would scarcely merit the sacrifice of time and the large space it would necessarily occupy. This laborious calculation would be, moreover, of little *practical* value, from the fact that the 14 cents "per capita tax" would sometimes amount to less than $15 assessment per year, whilst the law lately adopted by the Constitution Grand Lodge precludes any rate which would produce less than that amount.

The readers of this study will therefore prefer

to take my word for it that said calculation
proves: that the present "per capita tax" of 14
cents would be sufficient, not only "for the benefit of those brethren who may depart this life
within the next ten years" but for the next
twenty years; and this without assuming any
accession of young members, thus advancing the
age annually one year, and diminishing the
number surviving at the rate established by the
American Table of Mortality. During the first
ten years the assessment would increase with the
growing mortality to nearly $18.00 (to 128
deaths at 14 cents), and the reserve fund, from
surplus, (so-called) and from interest at 5 per
cent, to over half a million dollars. At the end
of the 20th year $1,120,000 would have been
paid out to the Wfdows and Orphans or designated beneficiaries of our brethren, of District
No. 1, who may have died during that period,
but then, in the 21st year not a dollar would be
left of that reserve fund, yet about 6100 members surviving, whose average would be beyond
sixty, their mortality over 200, while their payments, in death-assessments, restricted to 1½
per cent of that number, would produce about
$67.000 only scarce enough for one third of the

Endowments which would become due in that year.

Would not an increase of the "per capita tax" to 15 cents on each members' death, up to 1½ per cent, taking into account the admission of new members, replacing those lost by death and lapses, be sufficient? And would not this secure annual assessments amounting to *not less than fifteen dollars.*

To determine whether this or that rate of assessment would secure stability to the Endowment fund requires something more than a mere expression of opinion—mathematical proof is necessary.

At each of our Grand Lodge meetings the most conflicting opinions have been expressed ; some asserting the present rate to be ample for the fulfilment of our promises and obligations, now and in the future ; others, seriously doubting the safety of the Endowment, fearing their payment to be productive of only further expense without any compensating benefit, and predicting an early and disgraceful failure. But neither side had figured out the matter ; they all simply " believed " and " supposed " and " thought " or " were told." One generally relies on the low rates held out as inducement by Assessment Life Associations, some of which are now, apparently, very prosperous ; the other judges from the high rates a person of the average age of our members would have to pay in any sound Life Insurance Company.

True, it seems to require but little arithmetic and not much good common sense to know, that to pay $1000 at the death of every member, their contributions should be equal to an amount which, accumulating at compound interest, would produce $1000 during the number of years they are expected to live ; and as the average age of our members in District No. 1 is 45 years, and the expected life duration at such age averages 24 years, $21.41 *per annum* is the amount which,—accumulating at 5 per cent. interest—would in 24 years produce $1000. It may, however, be claimed that this amount would not be enough, considering that the payment of Endowments for members who die prematurely must produce a loss whereby the accumulation is materially diminished. Nor can it be denied that the accession of new, younger members, produce considerable retardation in the advance of Age, and thereby affects the result. Careful calculation, wherein all these factors are taken into account, is therefore absolutely necessary to find the proper and mathematically correct remedy.

In an article which appeared in THE AMERICAN HEBREW of May 8th, (vol. 22, No. 13, p. 194,) under the heading *"Make it Optional,"* it is "taken for granted that the Endowment system, as now existing in District No. 1, is unsafe ; and that the promise to pay to the heirs of all of the 9000 members $1000 cannot be fulfilled ; that the tables of mortality used by the insurance companies are safe guides in this matter ; that the system of assessing all members alike, irrespective of differences in age, is mathematically inaccurate and unjust. All this is admitted and has been fully shown in this study ; but the said article further asserts, that it would require a rate, determined by the average age of the members, "such as the poor men would be un-able to pay and the young men would be un-willing to pay, as they could secure cheaper insurance in safe insurance companies." This is *not* correct.

A uniform annual rate of $18, equal to 5 cents per day—which is the rate adopted in District

No. 2—is not beyond the ability of any poor man, and is a lower rate than any safe Life Insurance Company would charge for an insurance of $1000 to a person above the age of 32. And the young men of that District express themselves quite willing to pay this rate ; they opposed a reduction to $15 as asked by some *old* members; the young men cheerfully contribute the $3 more for the benefit of their old brothers' widows and orphans, for whose benefit they would be taxed were there no Endowment Fund.

The young members of District No. 1 will scarcely be less charitably inclined, much less would they withdraw from the Order for the sake of $3 per year, or 1 cent per day more than their own age alone might require, provided they could thereby secure the safety and permanency of the Endowment.

The advice to "Make the Endowment optional" will not prevail, if the question be properly considered how the duty of providing for and assisting the widows and orphans of our brethren could best be performed. This duty is imperative and inalienable.

Wolf's resolution, adopted and made law by the Constitution Grand Lodge, never contem-

plated "leaving the Endowment optional with
such lodges or members as may desire to participate." It merely left it to the option of each
District Grand Lodge to have or not have an
Endowment system. The proposed Endowment
Law, endorsed by a resolution of said Constitution Grand Lodge, recommended that partici
pation be made optional *for young unmarried*
men, until they either got married or reached
the age of 35. This seems the utmost extent
for a practically safe and just optional feature.
It would at the same time obviate the complaint
that members below the age of 32 are charged
too high a rate, and those who would leave the
Order for this reason—would be no loss. The
Grand Lodge might also permit those who consider the tax of $18 too burdensome, to pay half
that rate only for the proportionate part ($500)
of the benefit.

The TABLES herewith presented show that—
assuming the well established rates of mortality
and other factors, hereinafter explained—an enduring solution of the Endowment problem may
be reached at the rate of $18 per annum, and
that even a 15 cts. per capita tax would probably
not result in deficiency for many years to come.

TABLE I.

Showing how the Endowment Fund of District No. 1, I. O. B. B. would accumulate under a 15 Cents per capita tax, limited to $18.00 per annum when said tax begins to exceed that amount; and increasing the assessments after 30 years to $20.00 annually (assuming the probabilities explained in the text).

Year.	Age.	Mortality (death rate) in 1000.	Deaths.	15 Cents per capita to $18.00.	Amount of Annual Assessments.	Endowments to be Paid.	Surplus, 17 years, then Deficit.	Interest at 5 per cent.	Reserve Fund at end of year.
Jan. 1885.					from 9250 members.			On hand:	On hand: $169,000
1	45.0	11.2	104	$15.60	$144,300	$104,000	$40,300	$8,450	$217,750
2	45.7	11.4	105	15.75	145,690	105,000	40,690	10,887	269.327
3	46.4	11.7	108	16.20	149,850	108,000	41,850	13,466	324.633
4	47.1	12.0	111	16.65	154,010	111,000	43,010	16,236	383,879
5	47.8	12.4	115	17.25	159,560	115,000	44,560	19,193	447,632
6	48.5	12.8	118	17.70	163,720	118,000	45,720	22,381	•515,733
7	49.2	13.2	122	18.30	169,300	122,000	47,300	25,786	588,819
8	49.8	13.6	126	18.00	166,500	126,000	40,500	29,440	658,759
9	50.4	14.0	130	18.00	166,500	130,000	36,500	32,937	728,196
10	51.0	14.5	134	18.00	166,500	134,000	32,500	36,409	797,105

No.									
11	51.5	15.0	138	18.00	166,500	138,000	28,500	39,855	865,460
12	52.0	15.4	142	"	"	142,000	24,500	43,280	933,240
13	52.5	15.9	147	"	"	147,000	19,500	46,662	999,402
14	53.0	16.5	152	"	"	152,000	14,500	49,970	1,063,872
15	53.5	17.0	158	"	"	158,000	8,500	53,193	1,125,565
16	54.0	17.5	162	"	"	162,000	4,500	56,278	1,186,343
17	54.5	17.9	166	"	"	166,000	500 Deficit	59,317	1,246,160
18	55.0	18.6	172	"	"	172,000	5,500	62,308	1,302,968
19	55.5	19.2	177	"	"	177,000	10,500	65,148	1,357,616
20	56.0	19.9	184	"	"	184,000	17,500	67,880	1,407,996
21	56.5	20.6	190	"	"	190,000	23,500	70,399	1,454,895
22	56.9	21.2	196	"	"	196,000	29,500	72,744	1,498,139
23	57.3	22.0	203	"	"	203,000	36,500	74,906	1,536,545
24	57.7	22.6	209	"	"	209,000	42,500	76,827	1,570,872
25	58.1	23.2	215	"	"	215,000	48,500	78,543	1,600,915
26	58.5	23.9	221	"	"	221,000	54,500	80,045	1,626,460
27	58.8	24.4	226	"	"	226,000	59,500	81,323	1,648,283
28	59.1	24.8	230	"	"	230,000	63,500	82,414	1,677,197
29	59.4	25.5	236	"	"	236,000	69,500	83,859	1,691,556
30	59.7	26.2	242	"	"	242,000	75,500	84,577	1,700,633

TABLE I.—*Continued.*

Year.	Age.	Mortality in 1000.	Deaths.	Lapses.	Remaining Members.	Annual Assessments at $20.00.	Endowments to be Paid.	Excess Paid or Deficit.	Interest at 5 per cent.	Reserve Fund at end of year.
Jan. 1915.					9250				On hand :	$1,700,633
31	60.0	26.7	247	93	8910	$181,600	$247,000	$65,400	$85,031	$1,720,264
32	60.8	28.2	251	89	8570	174,800	251,000	76,200	86,013	1,730,077
33	61.4	30.0	257	86	8227	167,970	257,000	87,030	86,503	1,729,550
34	62.0	31.3	257	82	7888	161,150	250,000	95,850	86,477	1,720,177
35	62.6	33.0	260	79	7549	154,370	260,000	105,630	86,008	1,700,555
36	63.2	34.5	260	75	7214	147,630	260,000	112,370	85,027	1,673,222
37	63.8	36.0	260	72	6882	140,960	260,000	119,040	83,661	1,637,842
38	64.4	38.0	261	69	6552	134,340	261,000	126,660	81,892	1,592,883
39	65.0	40.0	262	66	6224	127,760	262,000	134,240	79,644	1,538,287
40	65.6	42.0	261	62	5901	121,250	261,000	139,750	76,914	1,475,451

		Total			Members	unprovided,	and	Deficit	
41	66.2	44.0	259	59	5583	114,840	259,000	144,160	73,772	1,405,063
42	66.8	46.5	259	56	5268	108,510	259,000	150,490	70,253	1,324,826
43	67.4	49.0	258	53	4957	102,250	258,000	155,750	66,241	1,235,317
44	68.0	52.0	257	50	4650	96,080	257,000	160,920	61,765	1,136,142
45	68.5	54.5	253	47	4350	90,000	253,000	163,000	56,802	1,029,944
46	69.0	57.0	248	43	4059	84,090	248,000	163,910	51,497	917,531
47	69.5	59.5	241	41	3777	78,360	241,000	162,640	45,376	800,267
48	70.0	62.0	234	38	3505	72,820	234,000	161,180	40,013	679,100
49	70.5	64.5	225	35	3245	65,160	225,000	159,840	33,955	551,215
50	71.0	67.5	220	33	2992	62,370	220,000	155,630	27,560	423,125
51	71.5	70.0	209	30	2753	57,450	209,000	151,550	21,156	292,731
52	72.0	73.5	202	28	2523	52,760	202,000	149,240	14,636	158,127
53	72.5	76.5	193	25	2305	48,280	193,000	144,720	7,906	21,313
54	73.0	80.0	184	23	2098	44,030	184,000	139,970	1,065	.....
		Total	5818	1334	2098					$117,592

TABLE II.

Based on the same conditions as Table I., with the only difference that $18.00 annually are assumed as per capita tax from the beginning.

Year	Age.	Mortality in 1000	Deaths.	Annual Assessment at $18.00.	Endowments to be Paid.	Surplus, 17 years, then Deficit.	Interest at 5 per cent.	Reserve Fund at end of year.
		from	9250 Members.				On hand:	On hand:$169,000
1	45.0	11.2	104	$166,500	$104,000	$62,500	$8,450	$239,950
2	45.7	11.4	105	"	105,000	61,500	11,997	313,447
3	46.4	11.7	108	"	108,000	58,500	15,672	387,619
4	47.1	12.0	111	"	111,000	55,500	19,380	462,499
5	47.8	12.4	115	"	115,000	51,500	23,124	537,128
6	48.5	12.8	118	"	118,000	48,500	26,856	612,479
7	49.2	13.2	122	"	122,000	44,500	30,623	687,602
8	49.8	13.6	126	"	126,000	40,500	34,380	762,482
9	50.4	14.0	130	"	130,000	36,500	38,124	837,106
10	51.0	14.5	134	"	134,000	32,500	41,855	911,461

11	51.5	15.0	138	"	138,000	28,500	45,730	985,691
12	52.0	15.4	142	"	142,000	24,500	49,284	1,059,475
13	52.5	15.9	147	"	147,000	19,500	52,973	1,131,948
14	53.0	16.5	152	"	152,000	14,500	56,597	1,203,045
15	53.5	17.0	158	"	158,000	8,500	60,152	1,271,697
16	54.0	17.5	162	"	162,000	4,500	63,584	1,339,781
17	54.5	17.9	166	"	166,000	500 Deficit.	66,989	1,407,270
18	55.0	18.6	172	"	172,000	5,500	70,363	1,472,173
19	55.5	19.2	177	"	177,000	10,500	73,608	1,535,281
20	56.0	19.9	184	"	184,000	17,500	76,764	1,594,545
21	56.5	20.6	190	"	190,000	23,500	79,727	1,650,772
22	56.9	21.2	196	"	196,000	29,500	82,538	1,703,810
23	57.3	22.0	203	"	203,000	36,500	85,190	1,752,500
24	57.7	22.6	209	"	209,000	42,500	87,625	1,797,625
25	58.1	23.2	215	"	215,000	48,500	89,881	1,838,006
26	58.5	23.9	221	"	221,000	54,500	91,900	1,875,406
27	58.8	24.4	226	"	226,000	59,500	93,770	1,909,676
28	59.1	24.8	230	"	230,000	63,500	95,483	1,941,659
29	59.4	25.5	236	"	236,000	69,500	97,082	1,969,241
30	59.7	26.2	242	"	242,000	75,500	98,462	1,992,203

TABLE II.—Continued.

Year.	Age.	Mortality in 1000.	Deaths.	Lapses, 1 per cent.	Remaining Members.	Annual Assessments at $20.	Endowments to be Paid.	Excess Paid or Deficit.	Interest at 5 per cent.	Reserve Fund at end of year. (on hand: $1,992.203½).
31	60.0	26.7	247	93	8910	181,600	247,000	65,400	99,610	2,026,413
32	60.8	28.2	251	89	8570	174,800	251,000	76,200	101,320	2,051,533
33	61.4	30.0	257	86	8227	167,970	257,000	87,030	102,576	2,067,019
34	62.0	31.3	257	82	7888	161,150	257,000	95,850	103,350	2,074,519
35	62.6	33.0	260	79	7549	154,370	260,000	105,630	103,725	2,072,614
36	63.2	34.5	260	75	7214	147,630	260,000	112,370	103,630	2,063,874
37	63.8	36.0	260	72	6882	140,960	260,000	119,040	103,193	2,048,027
38	64.4	38.0	261	69	6552	134,340	261,000	126,660	102,401	2,023,768
39	65.0	40.0	262	66	6220	127,760	262,000	134,240	101,188	1,990,716
40	65.6	42.0	261	62	5901	121,250	261,000	139,750	99,535	1,950,501

(Remaining Members at start of year 31: 9250.)

41	66.2	44.0	259	59	5583	114,840	259,000	144,160	97,525	1,903,866
42	66.8	46.5	259	56	5268	108,510	259,000	150,490	95,193	1,848,569
43	67.4	49.0	258	53	4957	102,250	258,000	155,750	92,428	1,785,247
44	68.0	52.0	257	50	4650	96,080	257,000	160,920	89,262	1,713,587
45	68.5	54.5	253	47	4350	90,000	253,000	163,000	85,679	1,636,266
46	69.0	57.0	248	43	4059	84,090	248,000	163,910	81,813	1,554,169
47	69.5	59.5	241	41	3777	78,360	241,000	162,640	77,703	1,469,232
48	70.0	62.0	234	38	3505	72,820	234,000	161,180	73,461	1,381,513
49	70.5	64.5	225	35	3245	65,160	225,000	159,840	69,075	1,290,748
50	71.0	67.5	220	33	2992	62,370	220,000	157,630	64,537	1,197,655
51	71.5	70.0	209	30	2753	57,450	209,000	151,550	59,882	1,105,987
52	72.0	73.5	202	28	2523	52,760	202,000	149,240	55,299	1,012,046
53	72.5	76.5	193	25	2305	48,280	193,000	144,720	50,602	917,928
54	73.0	80.0	184	23	2098	44,030	184,000	139,970	45,896	823,854
55	73.5	83.5	175	21	1902	40,000	175,000	135,000	41,192	730,046
56	74.0	87.0	165	19	1718	36,200	165,000	128,800	36,502	637,748
57	74.5	90.5	155	17	1546	32,640	155,000	122,360	31,887	547,275
58	75.0	94.0	145	16	1385	29,310	145,000	115,690	27,363	458,948
59	75.5	97.5	135	14	1236	26,210	135,000	108,790	22,947	373,105
60	76.0	102.0	126	13	1097	23,330	126,000	102,670	18,655	289,090

This computation, though requiring a great deal of figuring, can be comprehended. examined and corroborated by any person familiar with ordinary commercial calculations. To facilitate a better understanding of these, however, a kind and careful consideration of the following explanatory remarks is solicited :

Under the laws of nature, heavenly ordained, there is no such thing as CHANCE,—the human mind, ignorant of the future, can merely draw conclusions from observations of the past, as to what the PROBABILITY or CHANCE may be hereafter. From observation we know that, to every individual, death is only a question of time; the Psalmist already observed "our years are three score and ten, etc." From a large field of long and continued observations we can compute how many out of a hundred thousand persons of a certain age will probably die within one year; but no mortal can say *who;* hence the probability becomes more and more uncertain as we may attempt to apply the proportion to a smaller number. But while there may be slight deviations from the death-rate when applied to about 9000 members only—it may be less in one year and more in another,—the mortality table may, on the whole, be safely relied upon.

In many cases, however, it would be very deceptive to assume that "what has happened in a large number of instances in the past, may be accepted as a fact to determine the average result of a series of coming events with precision." The most deceitful schemes of cheap insurance are built on such misleading assumptions.

The Tables presented in this study are arithmancies for District No. 1, based on no unfounded suppositions; and yet, their figures are merely *probabilities* which may be safely relied upon to prove realities.

Thus, the MEMBERSHIP, which at present is nine and a quarter thousand, is assumed to remain numerically unchanged for a long period. During the last 20 years our Order has increased from 5900 to 25000 members; from 1865 to 1880 the addition of new members in District No. 1, averaged about 380 annually; since 1880, however, the accession to our ranks diminished to such an extent that no one acquainted with the facts would now assume a continued large increase for the future. As has already been stated in the former pages of this study, "the history of every social organization

in the past has shown that there comes a time
when it is impossible to increase the membership;" but history further proves that all well
organized and properly managed associations,
established for good and legitimate purposes
and on a sound basis, are, for centuries, able to
fill the gaps, created by deaths and discontinu-
ance, and to replace them by new members.
Hence it would be deceptive to assume an increase of membership for the future, but it may
be considered as of the highest probability, that
new members will supply the places of those who
die and lapse. Should the membership increase,
this would not affect the result, except that the
limit of annual assessments, proposed in Table
I, would be reached sooner, and if that amount
($18) be deficient, the greater accession of new
members would but *delay* the failure.

The AGE, as shown in column 1 of both
Tables I and II, is computed on the said
probability of maintaining the present number
of members, replacing those who die and lapse
by new members.[13]

_____

13. It starts with age 45, this being the lowest estimate of
the present *average* age of the members of District No. 1.
It is probably nearer 46 years.

The fallacious assumption that the average age of our membership could always be maintained stationary by any probable "infusion of young blood" has been repeatedly confuted in this study; but it is *not* disputed that, by an increase in membership or by replacing those who die with younger members, the advance in *average* age would be proportionately RETARDED. Arithmetically calculated the result is as follows: If in one year out of 1000 members 12 die, whose average age is 55, and these are replaced by 12 new members whose average age is 30, there would be a gain of 12×25=300 years, reducing the advance during that one year from 1000 to 700 years, hence the average age would increase 7-10 instead of one whole year; if 17 die out of 1000 members, and are replaced by as many new members each about 30 years younger than those who died, the advance in average age would be reduced one half; and when the death-rate reaches 33 out of 1000, and those departing are replaced by members 30 years younger, then the average age may remain almost stationary. The substitution of new younger members for older ones who lapse would also serve to somewhat retard the advance in average age.

The RATE OF ASSESSMENT is assumed (in Table I, column 4) to be at first 15 cents per capita for every death. This is the rate most likely to be adopted by the Grand Lodge, were it only to comply with the law passed by the late Convention prescribing a minimum annual assessment of $15 for every one thous-- and dollars. In the seventh year, when the mortality will be about one and one quarter per cent, this rate would produce an annual assess- ment of $18; and in ten years the mortality will reach 15 out of 1000, or one and one half per cent (which is the limit of assessment in District No. 1), the annual assessment would then be $20. At this rate, and assuming the member- ship to continue undiminished, the Reserve fund would amount in 40 years, *at 5 per cent interest*, to nearly three million dollars ($2,988,300.). But this would be more than necessary, and we may well suppose that a demand to limit the annual assessments to $18 would become irre- sistible. Were the membership of District No. 1, to increase to 10,000, which is certainly possible, a mortality of but 1¼ *per cent* would already produce an annual assessment of over $18.

Table I, therefore, calculates the amounts of
assessments (shown in column 5) at $18 from
the eighth to the thirtieth year, and, deducting
therefrom the Endowments to be paid (column
6), it gives in column *seven* the difference—the
surplus received during the first half of that
period, and the excess paid during the second
half, when the Endowments will exceed the
revenue from assessments.

Table II, calculates the assessments at $*18*
from the beginning, and in all other respects it is
the same as table I.

The INTEREST on the reserve, earned each
year at *five* per cent[14] is shown in the *eighth*

---

14. The rate of interest has decreased, but 5 per cent are
still safely obtainable on real estate loans, as evidenced by
the income of the largest financial institutions of the East
derived from that source:

The MUTUAL LIFE of N. Y. earned in 1884 on gross
assets amounting to $103,583,301; interest etc.,
$5,245,060.

The EQUITABLE of N. Y. earned in 1884, on gross assets
amounting to $58,161,926; interest etc., $2,972,150.

The NEW YORK LIFE of N. Y., earned in 1884, on
gross assets amounting to $58,941,739; interest etc.,
$2,873,390.

The CONNECTICUT MUTUAL of Hartford, earned in 1884

column; and—deducting the Endowments paid from assessment and interest received during the same year, and adding the difference to the reserve of the preceding year,—the result is found in the ninth (9th) column; showing at the end of the 30th year in Table I, an accumulated reserve fund of $1,700,000; in Table II, one of nearly two million dollars.

Looking carefully at the annexed Tables, it will be seen at once that the amounts received from assessments, *in excess of Endowments to be*

---

on gross assets amounting to $53,430,033; interest etc., $2,794,578.

Loans on real estate security, carefully and judiciously made are the best mode of investments for our Reserve funds; no other form of property has such inherent strength and value, it is the foundation and source of all other values. Real property may, at times, not find a purchaser at any price, but in due time it rises to its proper place, and if the loan were judiciously made, at about half of what was a fair valuation, no loss is to be apprehended.

Some would prefer U. S. Bonds for the investments of our Endowment funds, a mode by far easier for its managers, undoubtedly safe and always convertible into cash. But they who favor such investments do not know what great difference the rate of interest would make in the required rate of assessment. This important factor is but too often overlooked or disregarded.

paid will be annually *decreasing*,[15] while the amounts derived from interest on the Reserve fund are annually *increasing*, hence the difference in the rate of interest would in time balance the apparently excessive difference in the rate of assessments.

Both tables further show that after 30 years the average age of 60, and the so-called stationary point would be reached, provided always that the membership remains numerically the same by continually replacing those who die and withdraw with a like number of new members, but if no new members were to join then the reserve-fund, however large, would soon decline with the decrease of membership and consequent natural increase in age and mortality. It might be assumed by some brethren that accessions of new members would never cease in our Order, as they never ceased, for centuries, among Free Masons. I do not question the perpetuity of our beloved Order,

---

15. The Endowments to be paid exceed the assessments at $18 in the eighteenth year, if the assessments were calculated at $21 it would take only *four* years longer, before the death-rate would exceed the annual receipts from assessments.

but I deem it possible, if not probable, that it may at some future time adopt a different system of providing for our Widows and Orphans. And it may come to pass—although $18 is a very low rate for insurance of $1000 on the life of persons above the age of 30, and though our youngest men are quite willing to pay in favor of their old brethren, remembering that they also hope to get old—it *may* occur, I say, that young lodges with new young members would prefer to form an Endowment scheme or a class of their own; and that from such or any other cause the winding up of the old Endowment fund may become necessary.

Finally it is thus only that the question can be solved, arithmetically, whether the seemingly very large reserve fund would be more than needed or insufficient to pay *every* Endowment as it would be required. Even admitting that there may never be a last member, I must assume a terminal point, as this presents me the means of solving the problem; of knowing whether my plan is correct or not;—just as the compass cannot make a circle without beginning and closing at some assumed point, though circles have no terminal points.

The second half of Tables I and II, from the 30th year on, are therefore calculated without assuming any further addition or contribution of new members.

The AGE (column 1) would then increase annually one year, were it not that, by the death of the oldest members, the advance in average age would naturally be somewhat less than one year, as shown in this column ;[16] and columns 2 and 3 give the mortality and number of deaths annually reached.

The LAPSES (column 4) come then also into account, as they are no longer assumed to be replaced by new members. Experience places the withdrawals and suspensions in our Order at about two of every hundred members annually but with old members who belonged for many years to the Order scarce one half the number of lapses can safely be assumed. The MEMBER-SHIP, annually diminished by deaths and lapses is given in column 5.

---

16. Deduct from 1000 at age 60=aggregate 60,000, the 26 who died in one year at average age 70=1820 years, and add 1 year from each of the surviving 974 members— their aggregate age will be 59,154 years being equal to age 60.8.

The annual ASSESSMENTS are advanced to $20. This increase of 50 cents per quarter year, would certainly not be objected to at that remote period, when the average age of the members would exceed 60 years, and the rate of interest may probably have declined to 4 per cent. The bubbles of cheap insurance of to-day will then all be exploded and these Tables will live and be acknowledged a safe guide, though its author be probably long among the dead. That $20 would then be absolutely required is proven by the figures in column 6[17]. On the other hand, an assessment of $18 annually from now on, as figured in Table II, may be relied upon as securing the permanent soundness of the Endowment fund in District No. 1 ; its reserve fund would, at the end of the 60th year be still sufficient to pay to *every* members' family the promised Endowment, and could from this time on relieve all its members above the age of 75 from further contributions; a measure much to be desired.

---

17. From the members who die and from those who lapse in the course of the year only about half of the dues can be collected, hence these are reckoned at $10, and those surviving and continuing at $20.

This mode of assessment, payable regularly at $1.50 each month, or $4.50 quarterly, is so very little above the rate at 15 cents for each death during the first years and would be soon more than $18 under the present limit of 1½ per cent mortality, that its adoption should certainly prevail. It has besides many other advantages which will be discussed hereafter.

I hope to have fully and satisfactorily answered the question propounded, as to what rates would be sufficient to make the Endowment fund of District No. 1 sound and enduring. I believe to have shown by figures, the most probable future results, as far as these can be foretold; by the light of science and experience, yet without pretending to be infallible, without professing to prophesy. I hope to have demonstrated that the apprehension lest our Order be unable to carry out its pledges to the widows and orphans of its members are almost groundless, that, notwithstanding the shortcomings of the past, in not sooner providing for an adequate reserve, the remedy was nearer and easier than many supposed;—that, spite of the advanced age of a large number of our brethren in this, the oldest District, a future annual assessment of $18, would be sufficient under circumstances most likely to prevail, that unless there be a *decline* in membership, this rate would be reached within a few years, even at a 15 cents *per capita* tax, and much sooner if the membership were to increase. A little reflection will thus reveal the fact that to *withdraw* from the Order would tend to aggravate, and not to remedy the evil, and that mutual self-interest, if not devotion to the general good, would dictate the constant maintenance and not the dissolution of our membership. That the latter may never again be used as a threat, is one among many other reasons why the adoption of a fixed contribution of $18 is far preferable to varying contributions based on after-death assessments.

Those brethren who still are not disposed to concede the necessity of adopting the rate of $18 per annum as Endowment dues, those who will neither study nor believe the figures herewith submitted for their examination, those who still think that a better and cheaper, yet, at the same time, safe and reliable plan of assessment Life-insurance could be devised— to those I would put these questions:

Can any plan furnish insurance at less than cost?

Can any society be less subject to "fraudulent claims" than our lodges?

Is there any association where you could be as sure that every dollar paid in will be used for no other purpose than to pay the just claims of our deceased brethren, as with our own chosen trustees?

Is there any Society or form of Life insurance that can be as economically managed as our Endowment Funds?

Certainly, whatever the defects of our Endowment system may be, no dishonesty or malappropriation of its funds could ever be charged to its trustees; no attempt at a fraudulent claim has so far ever been made, nor has any honest claim ever been resisted. The annual expense of management is about 30 cents per member! And yet, some of you may say that there are associations where the rates for men, 45 years of age, are less than I claim to be required.

Yes, I admit there are. Let me take the "Mutual Reserve Fund Life Association," of your great State of N. Y., the largest and most successful of all, as an instance, and show it to you in its true light. I will not question the correctness of its brilliant statements; I will admit the great energy and ability displayed in its management;—nor will I doubt that its funds are carefully and honestly managed;[18] I, will not even ask you to take into consideration the fact that it charges $10 admission fee and one year's annual dues for $1000, then $2 annual dues FOR EXPENSES after the first year; but I will show you, from its own documents and papers, that the rate must increase in future years, so as sooner or later to force its members to withdraw.

In a little book of "ENDORSEMENTS," issued by the Mutual Reserve Fund Life Association is one from the celebrated old actuary, Elizur Wright, Ex-Insurance Commissioner of Massachusetts,[19] wherein he says:

"Your assessment rates being loaded one—

---

18. Though some well-informed persons charge, that for every $1000 paid to members, $600 were paid to managers, and that no proper account of expenses is rendered in its reports.

19. Hon. Elizur Wright is a bitter opponent of the old system of life insurance and has done much to improve it. In one of his books he wrote: "Having been extensively used as a sort of stool pigeon, in years gone by, when my attention was more directed to the value of the bait than to the inconveniences of the trap, it is a penitential labor with me to let the public know what, in my judgment, the matter is with life insurance."

third above the American mortality, and increasing according to the scale with the ages, I regard as equitable and sufficient to provide for the death-claims in full, after reserving one fourth for the Reserve fund." And with regard to the assessments becoming large and oppressive to the insured in future years, he says: "As they outgrow the need of insurance they can *diminish* the amount insured, from year to year, *or retire* without loss, and let younger men take their places."

The rates of said association are graded according to age[20] and are based on the cost under THE NATURAL PREMIUM PLAN, of which this association is the leading exponent.

In the "Society Journal," a monthly issued

---

20. These rates are : at Age 25, \$1.00 ; at age 45, \$1.64

		"	30, \$1.10;	"	50, \$2.00
		"	35, \$1.24;	"	55, \$3.25
		"	40, \$1.44;	"	60, \$4.50
		"	65, \$7.00.		

Thus at age 45 ten assessments would cost \$16.40 and \$2.00 for expenses=\$18.40.

No assurance is given as to the number of assessments; it is merely claimed that "no more assessments will be called for than is required for the payment of the losses and providing for the Reserve fund."

under the auspices of that Company, you can find the '*Natural Premium system*' fully explained and compared with the *level* or, what it calls the artificial premium plans. I extract from its last Oc ober number the following:

"The man who insures his building against damage or destruction by fire, pays such a premium cheerfully, because he understands it to be the price of contingent indemnity and that, whether he encounters losses or not, he receives a full equivalent of protection in exchange. He will even continue to pay an annually increasing premium without protest so long as he is satis fied that the increase of rate [which at the age of 75 is $87.10 for one year?] is warranted by increase of hazard and the company's necessities."[21] ......"that the rapid increase of premium *at advanced ages* would deter men from

---

21. Knowing that these rates would force members to give up their insurance when they get old, Mr. B. S. Price says, in justification thereof, (in "THE GUARDIAN," a semi-monthly devoted to the interest of Assessment Life Insurance, April 25, 1885): "Insurances continued into old age and beyond the producing period of life, are as false and useless as insurances upon dilapidated, decayed and untenantabl e houses."

paying them, is an object not wholly without foundation."......"It will be observed that though the *natural* premiums increase in amounts every year, and more rapidly at the older than at the younger ages, they do not exceed the level premiums of the old system until after 30 years, (from the age of 30)." "The advantages of the *natural* premiums (upon which the system of the Mutual Reserve Fund Life Association is modeled, by the maintenance of an adequate reserve to insure equality of payments and by the calling in of premiums by periodical installments) are suffi· ciently obvious."

But it is also sufficiently obvious that the *natural* premium plan, increasing with age— however advantageous and equitable it may appear to some—is ill adapted to *fraternal* insurance.

Our Endowment system should *not* ask its old members to retire and let younger men take their places. Our Order may invite young men to join, and must protect them from paying for the deficiency of its older members; but it would never allure young, new members by offering to them "a gambler's chance of winning profits out of a loss of protection by their old, most needy brethren." Let business associations, offering cheap Life insurance, claim the "Tontine System" as one of their "Pillars of strength"; a truly fraternal, charitable organization demands that its members stand together as long as life lasts, stand by each other's families beyond the grave; brothers should be willing to pay for one another, *sharing the burden all alike;* the young paying even a little more than is necessary at their present age, in order that the old, who have paid for many years, and may have to pay during many more, should *not* be required to pay *higher* rates. By far the most preferable way would be, to altogether exempt brothers beyond the age of 75 from paying any further assessments, and this might be safely done after 20 years, if by virtue of a better rate of interest and a lower rate of mortality the reserve fund should have become proportionately larger than calculated in the preceding Tables.

I could proceed to prove the importance of IMMEDIATELY adopting the level rate of $18. *per annum* ; it being the lowest possible rate to secure an enduring Endowment system; it being the highest practicable rate under which it is probable to replace those who die and withdraw by new members ; its cheapness compared with the higher rates of regular Life Insurance Companies, and its advantages over a lower, yet annually advancing assessment ; but

"I scorn to tyrannize over the impatience of my reader."

Moreover, the vast majority of our brethren place but little confidence in the so-called co-operative insurance societies, and are by no means disputing the correctness of my figures [23] and arguments. They simply think that, as their present contribution of 14 cents *per capita* at each death is more than sufficient for paying the endowment of $1000, and adds about $30 000 to the reserve fund, it ought to be enough. They do not ponder on the future, do not reckon that a mortality of one and one-half per cent. out of the present membership of District No. 1, would be 138 deaths ; that at 14 cents assessments this would amount to $19.32, and that whenever the death rate should reach 1½

---

23. Fractions are omitted in my calculations, and there are some inaccuracies; but not sufficient to materially affect the result.

per cent., this amount would have to be paid in one year. This rate of mortality is sure to come soon, by the natural and inevitable advance of age, — without assuming the possible contingency of an epidemic ;—this also they do not consider ; and though our old lodges show an annual death rate of two and more per cent., they scarcely believe it ; or, if they do, prefer to leave the unpleasant task of further increasing the tax, to future times and representatives, or to that supreme legislative body—the Constitution Grand Lodge.

This latter was relied upon in District No. 1.

The chairman of the Widow and Orphan Committee said in his report (Jan. 25th, 1885. Proceedings 33d annual session of D. G. L. No. 1, page 103) :

"A godsend to some, it was a burden to none. The Endowment fund, in spite of all that is said to the contrary, is one of the most important adjuncts in the District, and we hope to see it secured beyond peradventure for all time to come. We have no doubt the ensuing General Convention of the Order will find the right method for its perpetuity, and therefore we will make no recommendations at this time "

The committee to whom this report was referred fully concurred in this opinion, and expressed "the hope that the convention of the Constitution Grand Lodge, which meets shortly, will endeavor to legislate upon this subject in such a manner that any doubts that may have heretofore existed in the minds of our brethren, as to the stability of the present Endowment law, may be absolutely and completely dispelled."

Before examining these endeavors to so legislate in the C. G. L. Convention, and before discussing the causes of its unsatisfactory results, as far as District No. 1 is concerned, let us review the condition of the Endowment fund in the other Districts, at the time preceding said convention.

In DISTRICT No. 2, the membership increased from 2709 in Jan., 1879, to 3070 in Jan., 1885 ; the assessments paid by each member amounted to $15 per annum and the rate of interest earned was fully 7 per cent., increasing the reserve fund annually by about $20,000, or about $7 for each member. No changes were made in its laws, except such as became necessary by the consolidation of the three degrees into one only, as ordained by the C. G. L. in 1879, and some amendments, proposed by the Trustees, with a view to improve the practical working of the plan and to perfect some of its details. The most important of these was the change in the mode of collection from twenty *post-mortem* assessments at 75 cents to ten regular monthly dues at $1.50 (from Feb. to Nov., both inclusive). This change was made to avoid the irregularity caused by the occurrence of many deaths in one month and none in another, while it was absolutely certain that no less than twenty deaths would occur during each year in a membership of 3000, whose age averaged over 45 years; they would sometimes occur already during the first eight months, while under the monthly rates the collection was evenly distributed over the year. In 1883 forty-seven members died (which is 15.4 out of a 1000 or over 1½ per cent.), and for the first time the endowments exceeded the assessment-receipts; it became also evident that the rate of interest declined and no new investments with first-class 7 per cent.

In view of these facts the question arose whether $15 per annum would be sufficient to

secure the enduring prosperity, the permanency
of the endowment institution. In the report of
the Executive Committee of the C. G. L. (1872-
1873) I had demonstrated that $15 per annum
from each member, their average age being then
about 35, and none above the age of 45 to be
admitted, would be exactly enough to establish
a permanent and reliable endowment fund; and,
after the Chicago Convention had blindly rejected the excellent proposition for a genera
endowment of the entire Order, District No. 2
established its own district endowment on that
basis. But this was calculated on 7 *per cent.*
interest. That the assumption of this rate was
at that time both reasonable and justifiable, is
proven by the fact that during more than ten
years the reserve fund of District No. 2 was
safely invested at a rate considerably ABOVE
SEVEN *per cent*; but NOW it became impossible to
do so at more than SIX per cent.

The bearing of this change on the annual rate
of contributions from each member is greater
than most people imagine; and yet every school-
boy almost could deduce from any compound
interest table what amount of annual deposit is
required at different rates of interest to purchase

$1000 in a given number of years. Take 24 year—being the number of years men of age 45 may on an average be expected to live—and you will find[24] that: At 7 per cent. $1 annually= $62.25 ; hence $16.00 annually = $1000.00. At 6 per cent. $1 annually=$53.86 ; hence $18.56 annually=1000.00. At 5 per cent. $1 annually=46.73; hence $21.40 annually=$1000. So that 1 per cent. difference in the rate of interest causes a difference of from $2.50 to $3. in the annual deposit required for $1000 in 24 years. Aside from this there comes into consideration the difference produced by one per cent. interest on the already accumulated funds, which will amonnt in 30 years to over a quarter million dollars on $150,000 present reserve.

The report of the Endowment Fund Trustees to D. G. L. No. 2 (Dec. 31, 1883) presented a

---

24. In some compound interest tables (wherein the deposit is not calculated *in advance*, at the beginning of each year) we find that $1 annually will amount in 24 years, at 7 per cent. to $58.18; at 6 per cent. to $50.81; at 5 per cent. to $44.50; hence for $1000 the annual deposit required would be—at 7 per cent. $17.18; at 6 per cent. $19.68; at 5 per cent. $22.47. The *difference* is the same !

Table showing arithmetically that, assuming 6 per cent. interest hereafter, $18 instead of $15 would be the proper annual assessment, and strongly recommended the adoption of this rate for the future, stating, at the same time, that this was not necessary for our old members, not lor those who will depart this life within 25 years, but for our young members, for those whom we expect to survive us.

This Endowment Trustees' report was referred, as usual, to a committee ; a majority of its members were at first opposed to the recommendation to increase the assessments, or desired that action thereon be at least postponed for a year, until the proposition could have been submitted to the lodges; but after a full and fair discussion they were converted by the strong arguments of the advocates, and more still, perhaps, by those of the opponents ; finally, all except one signed the majority report, which concurred in the recommendation of the Trustees and, in strong and most flattering expressions of satisfaction and confidence, endorsed the levying of sufficient assessments as the only honest method for providing against any possible failure of our solemn promises in the future.

The minority report of one recommended that action upon the proposed increase of assessment be deferred until the next annual meeting of the G. L. The consideration of these reports called forth much eloquence on both sides, and was participated in with considerable interest by nearly all the members present. Finally, the motion to approve the majority report was agreed to, and the proposed amendment was adopted by 42 votes in the affirmative, against 17 in the negative.

It is obvious that the endowment fund of District No. 2, with its proportionately larger reserve fund and its ability to earn 6 per cent. interest, was not near as much in need of adopting the rate of $18 as District No. 1 is. But by the adoption of that rate it has secured its endowment fund beyond all possible contingencies, independent of any accession or withdrawal of members and without ever requiring an increase of that rate, unless the rate of interest should decline below five per eent. investments on first-class real estate security in Cincinnati, Chicago, St. Louis, and other cities outside of the great money centres of the East, will most probably bring 6 per cent. interest for many years to come;

and, if so, District No. 2 will be enabled to relieve its members when they will reach the age of 75 from paying any further assessments. Thus another excellent feature would be added to our endowment system. If there be hereafter a surplus beyond the necessary reserve, by reason of a smaller mortality or a higher rate of interest than calculated upon, those members who will have contributed over 30 years will be justly entitled to that surplus. I consider it by far more important that old members, physically disabled to earn money, be relieved, than it is that our young members, able to work and earn, should save ONE cent per day, by paying now three dollars less ; and I am happy to find that our young brethren in District No. 2 do not in the least object to the increased rate of assessment.

There are some OLD deluded members who imagine that the seeming surplus is demanded for the benefit of future generations. It is quite useless to argue with these men ; their minds seem incapable to grasp the plainest calculations connected with the problems of life insurance; and it is quite unnecessary, in District No. 2 at least, as they are in a hopeless minority. For

this very reason Grand Lodge .No 2 wisely con-
cluded to allow these few opponents full freedom of speech, so that they could not complain
of being gagged by the majority. They found
themselves nevertheless overwhelmingly defeated, and the increase from $15 to $18,
adopted in May, 1884, was confirmed and endorsed with still larger majority by the Grand
Lodge in May, 1885.

In District No. 3, the subject of Endowment
was often brought before the consideration of
the Grand Lodge, but up to this day no reserve
fund was provided for. The members, 2937 in
number, pay an assessment of 35 cents at each
death, or about just enough to pay $1,000 to the
widow or orphans of the deceased brother. The
present mortality is 12 out of a thousand, indicat-
the age of 47 as the average. A few members
have been struggling year after year to have the
Endowment law amended, so as to provide for
a sinking fund; but were yearly defeated. The
proceedings of this District Grand Lodge 1884–
1885 contains the following report: "The General Committee of previous years have urged
upon the D. G. L. the necessity of creating a
reserve or surplus fund in some shape or form,

but always without success, and therefore it is useless again to submit similar views which this committee entertains and shares with its predecessors. . . . . We recommend the adoption of the proposed amendment, providing for a per–capita assessment of forty cents for each death and setting aside, as a reserve fund, whatever surplus may remain after the payment of the one thousand dollars. It has been urged as an objection to amending the Endowment laws, that the Convention of the Order, called to assemble in the city of New York on the first day of March 1885, may pass some general laws on the subject of endowment, rendering our action nugatory. . . . . . This possibility, however, should not interfere with your proceedings to-day, inasmuch as the question is properly before you and the anticipated action of the Constitution Grand Lodge altogether problematical." "Our laws are defective. . . . . Old laws once good (?) and efficient, become, as time advances and the world moves, inefficient and unadapted to existing demands. It is worse than folly to cling to old laws and regulations because of their age and because they were once (supposed to be) 'good enough,' and should therefore be

' left alone.' . . . . Our members are just so
many years older, without a perceptible increase
of young blood to infuse the necessary vitality.
These considerations certainly demand prudent
and wise legislation looking to the enaction of
laws that will ensure protection to those who
joined the Order of late years or who may hereafter unite with it."

A motion that the consideration of this proposition be postponed till after the convention of
the Constitution Grand Lodge was lost by 42
nays against 40 ayes.

A substitute, providing for a quarterly payment of 75 cents from every member into the
treasury of his Lodge, towards the formation of
a reserve fund, was first amended to fifty cents.
and then not receiving the necessary two-third
vote, though a majority, (43 ayes and 28 nays)—
was declared *lost*.

Here, then, we have a District where the assessments are very low as not to exceed, so far,
$12 per annum; during last decade the *total* ex-
pence of each member did not exceed $15 per
annum. It possesses since 1873 a nice and
commodious home—a B'nai B'rith Hall—where
peace and harmony exists "not only amongst

the members of the different Lodges, but also in relation of this Grand Lodge to its subordinates.

Did the Order increase there during the last years as heretofore? Let the last annual report of District No. 3 give us the answer.

The General Committee, after furnishing the statistical figures, says:

"The above exhibit again shows a continued decrease in our numbers. It is a humiliating fact to contemplate that there is so little interest taken to add new strength to our Order. During the last six years we have lost over eighty members, instead of increasing in numbers, which statement can be readily verified."

Here is evidence that a low rate of Endowment taxation does not increase the membership of our Order, nor even prevent their "dropping off." District No. 2 whose members paid the highest rates, accumulating a large reserve fund, has increased its membership whilst District No. 3 with the lowest taxation did not add to its members or to its funds. The members of both Districts feel, equally, a glow of pride and pleasure in the reflection that hundred thousands of dollars have been distributed in support of the families of their deceased brethren; but those of the one feel that their endowment system is safe and well secured, that it protects future members, young men who wish to join, from being taxed for the present old members;—while those of the other Districts feel more or less the insecurity or instability of their system.

The average age of our brethren in District No. 3 is somewhat more advanced than in any other District, and *no* reserve fund has been allowed to accumulate,[25]—consequently assessments at the rate of $15 per annum would have to be raised to $18 and to $20 within ten years to make good the error of the past and secure the stability of the endowment for the future. Were this District to continue under its present plan, of paying just enough to produce $1000 at each death, its members would also be required to pay annually increasing amounts, and this without limit, as the mortality will increase with advancing age; and it would make but very little difference whether the membership remain about the same or continue to decrease.[26]

---

[25] On January 1st, 1885 it had a balance of $2886.

[26] When the age of 56 is reached, the rate of mortality

The lowest rate to secure a permanent endowment for District No. 3 is $18 for one thousand dollars annually, provided that 6 per cent interest can be obtained on the investment of its reserve. This rate of interest may, probably, be safely obtainable, if the Trustees were not restricted to loans in Philadelphia, but permitted to lend on property of double value in other cities, such as Pittsburgh, Wheeling, Newark, &c.

From past experience it seems doubtful that $18 could be carried in the D. G. L., or that any higher rate than $15, being the lowest rate permitted under our Constitution, could prevail. But it would be *better* to reduce the endowment to $500, making the tax $9 annually, than to promise twice that amount for $15. An endowment of 500 which is SURE is by far more valuable than one of $1,000 which is a DELUSION. The aggregate lodge dues would thus be re-

---

being 2 per cent, there would then die about sixty out of three thousand members; the assessments at 35 cents would amount to $21 per year. Were the number to decrease to, say, 2,600 members it would require assessments at 40 cts, and although 52 or 53 only would then die in one year, the tax would amount to the same and would continue to increase from year to year.—The result need not be told.

duced instead of being increased; you will get new young members, and members who do not join for the sake of the Endowment. Let these and all who hanker after *cheap* insurance get it elsewhere. You might then also allow young, unmarried men, to join your Lodges without contributing to the Endowment fund, until they get married.

This is what District No. 3 should do. I would have much preferred to tell you that "with some zeal you might be able to secure an increase of membership, and increased benefits; that you might keep down the death rate at about one per cent forever"—as others have told you before. It would be pleasanter to tell you what you like to hear, than to tell you what you need. But sweet deceiving flattery brings mischief and ruin, while truth,—though bitter, brings life and prosperity.

IN DISTRICT No. 4, the Pacific coast,—the members protest with remarkable unanimity and with incomprehensible bitterness against any interference with their Endowment. The lodges comprising this District sent a delegation to the General Convention held at Philadelphia in 1879, who presented their protest and a petition

" to refrain from the passage of any law altering
the present status of the Endowment system,
and to 'leave well enough' alone. "—" Fearing
that the advocates of the INJUDICIOUS measure
—to establish a GENERAL ENDOWMENT SYSTEM
—might renew their attempt in that direction,"
they claimed the right to administer their financial affairs as they deem best. And what did
those advocates of a General Endowment do?
Convinced that "laws and reforms however
wise and just, cannot be carried out successfully
while they are obnoxious to a great majority of
those for whom they are intended," they reported : "We deem it against the wishes of a
majority of the fraternity as well as inexpedient,
at this time, to enact a general Endowment law."
They merely recommended : "that the various
Districts endeavor to improve their laws so as to
give stability and permanence to the mode of
supporting the widows and orphans of our deceased members." They merely recommended,
as a necessity, the establishment of adequate
Reserve funds ; and they expressly stated : "We
do *not* recommend that this Constitution Grand
Lodge exercise its supreme legislative power in
prescribing limits of benefit or other rules to the

various Districts on the subject of Endowment, hoping tnat the Grand Lodges may each enact such wise laws for the protection of the widows and orphans as will conduce to the welfare of their sections."

This, certainly, proves that the fears of the California Lodges were unfounded; but so also were the hopes of the Constitution Grand Lodge that adopted the report.

In 1880 District No. 4 had 1642 members; during that year the mortality was 16, and the assessments levied were 60 cents per capita, scarcely sufficient to produce $1,000 at each death. Nevertheless, in the following year, this District Grand Lodge adopted a resolution which raised the Endowment to $2,000, and the assessments for each death to $1.25 per capita. This movement was founded, no doubt, on the exceptionally small mortality of 1881,—there being *five* deaths only out of its 1724 members.

Brother Heineman, member of the Executive Committee for that District, wrote in his report for 1882 as follows: "The majority of the Past Presidents of this District have not yet, and probably never will, acknowledge the necessity of acquiring and accumulating an adequate

sinking fund to protect our Endowment system.
. . . They even go so far as to use the interest of our fund, which has now reached the
respectable sum of $47,000, to defray an addi-
tional assessment whenever there should be
enough acquired to do so (to pay $2,000). This
is altogether wrong according to my idea ; yet I
am positive there are not more than ten members in our entire District Grand Lodge, out of
a total of three hundred, to share my opinion."
" This point ought to be one of our main issues
at the next Constitutional Convention, and all
District Grand Lodges should be held to levy a
certain *pro rata* at each assessment, for the purpose of acquiring adequate sinking funds."
And now, when the Constitution Grand Lodge
finally has done, what California's own representative said ought to be done—a cry of dissatisfaction is raised ; open rebellion is seriously
threatened. The members of District No. 4
ask, why should we be so heavily taxed, that the
distant future may be provided for ! Like the
Hibernian orator they cry : " Why should we
care for posterity ? What has posterity done for
us ?"

The simplest calculation would prove that,

far from providing for "the distant future" or for "posterity," they fail to provide for one-half of their members, for those who would still be living about twenty years hence. These will then have reached the age of 60, and some of 70 years, consequently a mortality of 4 per cent., requiring 40x$2,000=$80,000 annually, $80. from each one of the one thousand surviving members. But such calculation is denounced as erroneous, as it does not take into consideration the probability that young members would fill the places of those who die, etc. In other words : they are unwilling to pay for posterity, but are most willing to let posterity pay for them. They expect this as "a matter of course;" just as we know that for every death there is also at least one birth.

What do the facts show in District No. 4?

1. That up to January, 1885, it paid 98
    Endowments, amounting to . $124,000

2. That these 98 deceased mem-
    bers contributed $6,900

3. That 302 suspended members
    contributed 10,000
    ————— 17,657

Leaving a deficit as to surviving —————
members of $106,343

At the present amount of Endowments —
$2,000—this deficiency would increase from year
to year, and would, before many years, have to
be paid by future members, by posterity, or
could not be paid at all. Is it not evident that
young men would soon begin to understand
this and would *not* join? Some understand it
already.

In 1884, the President of District Grand
Lodge No. 4 (Bro. B. F. Sperling) avowed that:
"by careful study of the subject, from the interest he felt in the ability of the Order to maintain
its integrity, HIS VIEWS HAD MATERIALLY
CHANGED. He had formerly made a recommendation, which had been adopted, viz.: to
use the surplus received from assessments for
the payment of an Endowment whenever the
amount of such excess reached $2,000. He
would now suggest and advise that all monies
so received be permitted to accumulate for
future exigencies. He was convinced, that if
the present system were to remain in force, the
promise to pay $2,000 to the heirs of a deceased
brother would after a time, from the very nature
of things, be found impossible of fulfillment ;
. . . that unless some method, other than

the one now in use, be found, the future would present a sad commentary on human credulity and human thoughtlessness. . . . That the fact, that the Order was pledged to pay the Endowment to the heirs of every member, must not be overlooked ; and that a failure to do so would bring disruption and dissolution " To avoid any of these possible calamities, he submitted two propositions to the Grand Lodge : One, to make a uniform annual assessment, sufficient in amount to *insure* the payment of the Endowment. The other, to segregate the Endowment fund from the direct control of the District Grand Lodge. POSSIBLY IT MIGHT BE WISE TO COMBINE BOTH PROPOSITIONS.

His recommendations were NOT approved by the Grand Lodge, except as to the appointment of a special committee on this subject, which was to report to the next annual session.

In 1885, the same President (having been re-elected) again referred to the thoughts he had expressed in his former annual message and stated that many members of the Grand Lodge had regarded him as an alarmist. But, since he had spoken upon that subject, our eminent Grand President of the Order, Brother Julius

Bien, had expressed his views upon the Endowment question,[27] so full of anxious apprehension
and so fraught with wisdom, that he quoted
them in full, saying that "notes of warning
from a source so much entitled to our respectful
consideration, ought not to pass unheeded."
In view of the near approach of the extra session of the Constitution Grand Lodge, (to convene in New York in March, 1885) he said in
his Message : " It is a question which ought to
be settled authoritatively by the Constitution
Grand Lodge in such a manner that the rule of
action should be uniform throughout the Order,
and that the principles upon which the Endowment system shall be conducted will be established on a basis, so wise, as to avert any possible calamity in our Order, even in the far
future."

Grand Lodge No. 4, however, adopted a resolution "that we desire NO CHANGE in our
Endowment laws, as at present constituted ;
that we find them working satisfactorily and
desire NO legislation on the matter of Endow-

---

27. Report of the Executive Committee 1883–1884."
" Introductory;" pages 3 and 4.

ment which will affect District No. 4." A committee was also appointed to draft resolutions in conformity with this sentiment, urging the lodges to submit them to the Constitution Grand Lodge. They did so, and not a single lodge of District No. 4 dissented.

Thus it is apparent that the majority of its members still believe that their death rate will not materially increase ; they rely on the salubrious climate of the Pacific coast, on its immunity from yellow fever and, perhaps, from other epidemics ; they persistently ignore that, nevertheless, they will all die, and that their average duration of life differs but very little from that of the Atlantic coast. They still consider the accumulation of a large reserve fund impracticable and unnecessary—though every one of them, individually, wishes and tries to accumulate wealth. They consider a tax of $15. per annum burdensome, and yet boast that they will be willing and ready to pay twice and thrice that amount of assessment in later years, if necessary ; forgetting that many members may then not be *able* to pay about $4. monthly, (as the members of the Mutual Covenant Endowment Association of Cincinnati, O., are now required to pay) and that, certainly, no young men would then be willing to join.

Now, if the members of District No. 4 prefer to be guided by leaders of certain so-called Mutual Aid Societies who are unknown and irresponsible to them, rather than by the chosen representatives of their own Order,—let them get their insurance in those societies, or from an insurance association of their own *outside of the Order*, as is done by Masons and Odd-fellows. Every District is perfectly at liberty to have or not have an Endowment institution. All that our Constitution demands is : that no Endowment system be carried on in the honored name of the Order B'nai B'rith which might fail in the fulfillment of its promises and obligations. If our brethren want to carry on a Widow and Orphan Endowment, *as a part of our noble institution and under its jurisdiction*, it must be an honest one ; not what is proven to be a delusion that would end in disaster and disgrace.

What cause, then, is there for protests or for revolutionary measures? If I am allowed to give advice or to make a suggestion, it is this : Combine both propositions made by your President in 1884. Let District Grand Lodge No. 4

enact an Endowment law, in harmony with the late constitutional enactment, for $1,000 only, fixing the contributions at $15. annually, giving to unmarried men the option not to contribute nor participate, until they get married, and let those who desire an additional insurance of $1,000 or more dollars form a separate, optional organization, under any plan or system they may deem proper, apart from the control and responsibility of the District Grand Lodge and of the Order.

IN DISTRICT No. 5, an Endowment law was adopted in 1874. It gave to the widow, orphans or designated beneficiary of each deceased member $1000, to be produced by assessment; and it established a sinking fund, formed on a basis of 15 cents per member at each death. This fund was to be kept under the control of the several lodges, and from it all assessments in excess of twenty deaths were to be paid.

Thus the study of this District Endowment— of its struggles for more than ten years—offers an opportunity for considering the question as to whether it were better for each lodge to be the custodian of its own share in the reserve fund, or whether it would be more advisable to centralize it and vest its management and custody in one Board of Trustees. Theoretically, it makes no difference which of the two methods is adopted, if the amount be the same, and if it be equally well guarded and invested at interest. Fears of possible misnuanagement, petty distrust or local considerations induced men in this and every other District to oppose centralization ; but, practically, this method is by far safer and more advantageous. It is easier to find a few men possessing the necessary business capacity, combined with strict integrity, who will take charge of a large fund and will consider it an honor and a sacred duty to do so; while, among thirty or more lodges, mistakes will sometimes be made in the selection of so great a number of Trustees—three from each lodge. Besides, small amounts cannot be as safely invested, often not at all, and losses become inevitable.[28]

------

28. In 1878 already, Malachi Lodge, No. 146, reported the fact that $360.22 of their Endowment sinking fund had been lost by the failure of a bank, and asked whether the lodge or the trustees were responsible for the loss. The General Committee decided that the Grand Lodge can hold only the lodge responsible for keeping the Endowment

Other difficulties and complications arise from the divided administration of the fund into many small fractional parts, as will be fully illustrated by the developments in District No. 5.

During the first years the members of this District were not only well satisfied, but quite enthusiastic about their endowment system. In 1876 it had been visited—at Savannah, Ga.—by that dreadful scourge, the yellow fever. The suffering and destruction among the inhabitants of that section was great, yet the deaths were only 23 out of the 2028 members composing the 32 lodges that formed that District; and on October 1, 1877, the amount of the reserve was already $24,382.71, while $25,000 had been paid for endowments during that year. Nevertheless, amendments were offered and made at every

---

sinking fund intact, and can not know the trustees in this matter. Malachi Lodge appealed; claiming that " the trustees could not be compelled to pay the same, having deposited the money in a chartered bank—nor the lodge, having strictly complied with the law, it would be unjust to expect us to pay the amount again." In vain did the General Committee urge the adoption of measures placing the fund more directly under the control of the Grand Lodge.

meeting of the Grand Lodge, and more stringent measures adopted for their administration.

In Jan., 1878, the President's report to the Grand Lodge states that quite recently the General Committee directed him to suspend the charters of three lodges for non-payment of their endowment dues. In the same message the President said: "The only safety and surety for the perpetuation of the endowment is in the strict enforcement of that part of the law creating a sinking fund. . . . Is there a sane man who would insure his life in a company whose receipts only equal its annual disbursements? . . . I warn you, my brethren, as you value the *endowment*, do not give up your sinking fund."

And yet, in 1879, his successor states to the Grand Lodge : " In consequence of the excellent health in the District, and not a single death during the first six months of the current year, many of the lodges took advantage of this Providential blessing, by adopting laws tending to the ultimate destruction of the sinking fund."

In 1880, repeated complaints were expressed against several of the lodges, they having been in arrears for two and three assessments at a time, and asserting that "the law now in force does not serve the purposes for which it was designed." The General Committee's report makes the following statement: " By our present law the custody of the fund is entrusted to the lodges, but the same law also makes it the duty of a certain set of officials to receive this fund from the lodge, to invest it and to be responsible for its safe keeping. ˉ It is true, they are required to give bond for the faithful execution of this trust, but, aside from the fact that such bonds are generally of insufficient security, and the manifest impossibility of the Grand Lodge satisfying itself of the sufficiency of 175 bonds, scattered over and subject to the varying laws of five States and the District of Columbia, they cannot be enforced and the penalty collected without expensive and tedious litigation." To remedy this and other defects of the law, the General Committee submitted a set of carefully prepared amendments, proposing to assimilate this law with that of District No. 2, changing the occasional assessment to a fixed contribution, and placing the management of the Endowment sinking fund in the hands of one board of control, to be elected by the Grand Lodge.

But the Special Committee on Endowment recommended some temporary changes only, and a *Resolution* : " That this committee be continued with authority to draft a plan for a revised Endowment Law, if deemed necessary, and that they submit their report to the secretary of the Grand Lodge ninety days before the next meeting of this Grand Lodge, which officer shall submit the same to the lodges of the District for their approval or disapproval, sixty days before such session, when if approved by a two-third majority of all the lodges, and so reported to this Grand Lodge, the same shall be declared a law." This was, of course, adopted. With what result ?

The Endowment Law and its proposed modifications were widely discussed in all the lodges —discussed by men who have very little knowledge and a mere superficial understanding of the subject. And when the Grand Lodge of District No. 5 met in January, 1881, it again adopted the worse than useless Resolution, that the further consideration of the subject of Endowment be postponed until the next annual session and that the secretary be instructed to have printed a sufficient number of the reports of the majority and minority of the Endowment Committee, together with the proposition of Rimmon Lodge, No. 68, with such other matter as may be presented, and that in due time such information be forwarded to the several lodges.

In vain had the worthy president of the District Grand Lodge urged immediate action, as follows : " I recommend to your favorable consideration the amendments to the Endowment Law proposed by the special committee. I am prompted to do so because I believe a change of the existing law absolutely essential, in order to secure a prosperous future for our institution. . . . If the present system shall be continued, it can be demonstrated with mathematical precision that early in the next century the heirs of members must be deprived of their promised legacies. This result is the inevitable sequence of the action of the spend-thrift, who improvidently lavishes more than his income, and in a few years becomes bankrupt.

Taking the past decade for our guidance we must admit that if the present law remains intact, the death assessments will be multiplied until they will become a heavy burden, and thereby prevent an infusion of youthful blood into the infirm body. . . . It is therefore our duty to enact a law that will improve the present system, and arrest the future danger that threatens to weaken the resources and strike at the vitality of the Order." . . .

"Recent irregularities and violations of law by some of our lodges in the mode of accounting and investing this fund, and the dilatory action of other lodges in transmitting the assessment for deaths, prove that its transfer to the Grand Lodge would not only be most judicious, but highly advantageous from every point of view. It would then become a sacred trust fund, the account of which would be correctly kept and promptly rendered ; each member would know the exact amount he was required to pay ; the assessments would then be promptly settled, the principal and interest invested in accordance with law, each year swelling its volume, until it shall have augmented to such a sum that the interest accruing therefrom will materially decrease the future taxation of each member of the District."

"I can present no stronger argument in support of the proposed law than to state that a similar system has obtained in District No. 2, where it has been in practical operation with most favorable results for the past seven years. . . . The experience of a sister jurisdiction, where the plan has been fairly and favorably tested for several years, is an exhaustive argument in its favor."

But the representatives did not listen to arguments. They preferred to refer the subject to their constituents — to the "sovereign lodges."

It is the curse of democratic governments that the most ignorant people claim equal suffrage in determining all questions, regardless of the degree of knowledge they possess—regardless of other qualifications which an intelligent and able consideration may require. They are free men, hence they deem it their prerogative to decide what they wish or wish *not* to do, they will not concede that others may know better what they *should* do. The more intelligent among the people expect and demand of their representative that he fully inform himself and decide in his wisdom, according to his honest conviction, what is best for the people. But most representatives prefer *not* to take this responsibility ; they hesitate in adopting measures

of whose excellence and justice they are sure,
simply because they have no faith in the intelligence of the majority of their constituents, and
are swayed more by their fear of the noisiest
and most ignorant of these, than by a longing
for the silent praise of the best and wisest men,
or of their own conscience.

Is it to be wondered then, that the average
member, seeing his chosen representative waver-
ing, disregarding the voice of science and the
lessons of experience, coming home to ask for
instructions, instead of teaching—is it to be
wondered then, that the people lend their ear to
fallacies, and do not recognize them as such
until they have to suffer from their bad results?
Goethe lets his Mephisto truly say :

"Verachte nur Vernunft und Wiſſenſchaft
Des menſchen allerhöchſte Kraft,
Laſſ nur in Blend-und Zauber werken
Dich von dem Lügengeiſt beſtarken—
So hab' ich dich ſchon unbedingt."

Thus year after year passed away without
bringing about the much-desired and much-
needed reform in District No. 5.

In the year 1881, however, an alarming death-
roll aroused the members to the importance of

this matter. There had been no epidemic. From purely natural causes thirty·one members (nearly 15 in a thousand) had died during that year, and the District was compelled, under the then existing law, to use considerable of the sinking fund. Difficulties arose in drawing on the different lodges for the proportionate share of the fund held by each of them. Circulars had to be issued by the general committee recommending the lodges to abstain from making investments, and the President found it necessary to have the securities of the Endowment sinking fund examined and to give special instructions not to install the trustees of any lodge whose accounts were not kept in accordance with the law.

In order to induce the lodges to consent to a centralization of the sinking fund, the Endowment committee proposed that each lodge surrender the small sum of $7 for each of its members, but Eliah Lodge, No. 50, proposed to amend even this to *two* dollars only.[29] Neither proposition, however, prevailed.

---

29. On Jan. 1st, 1882, the District had 2270 members, and the Endowment sinking fund was reported to amount to $48,547, equal to nearly $22 for each member.

In view of the experienced great increase in mortality, however, an amendment was adopted providing for quarterly endowment dues of $3.75, payable to the trustees of the lodge. These should invest the surplus in U.S. bonds, to be registered as follows : *"Endowment sinking fund of District Grand Lodge, No. 5, I. O. B. B., subject to the order of*————*Lodge, No.*————, *I. O. B. B.*

But the registering officer of the U.S. Treasury Department immediately observed that this form of issue leaves the control of the bonds in doubt; and he ruled against this form. In his letter of Nov. 27th, 1882, he wrote to Dr. S. B. Wolfe, secretary of the D. G. L. : "Assuming that the bonds belong to the sinking fund of the Grand Lodge, I am of the opinion that trustees should be appointed (if there are now none), and the bonds should be inscribed : '*The trustees of the Endowment sinking fund of District Grand Lodge, No. 5, I. O. B. B.*'"

Many other difficulties presented themselves under this system,[30] and the President felt justi-

---

30. Hasmonea Lodge, No. 45, had $5000 of the Endowment sinking fund invested in 4 per cent. U. S. bonds, and afterwards had these converted into a $3\frac{1}{2}$ per cent. certifi-

fied in declaring to the G.L. session in February, 1883, that "the working of this law, on its present plan, has not been satisfactory." Hasmonea Lodge instructed its representatives to that G.L. session *for*: "centralization of Endowment fund; each lodge contributing one-half of its present sinking fund, and the other half to flow back into the lodge fund of each lodge."

The committee on Endowment presented a report, submitting an entirely new Endowment law, wherein the assessments were reduced to $13 annually; the management and investment of the funds were to be entrusted to a board of trustees, composed of thirteen past presidents of lodges of this District. The securities and moneys then held by the lodges, as custodians of the Endowment sinking fund were to be surrendered to the said board of trustees, elected under this law, and to be invested by said board

---

cate, at a profit of about $600. The lodge held the amount so gained as a portion of its lodge fund, claiming that the Grand Lodge had no authority to inquire into the matter, but must be satisfied. The general committee, on the contrary, claimed that all profits, premiums or interest derived from investments of the Endowment sinking fund must accrue to this fund and be so accounted for.

of trustees in U. S. securities, and registered in the name of: *" The Trustees of the Endowment sinking fund of District No. 5, I. O. B. B."* (as suggested by the U. S. Reg.)

To make this law the more acceptable, or, as the committee expressed it, "to meet the views and wishes of the entire brotherhood in this District," it further recommended that each lodge be exempted from the payment of Endowment dues from the 1st of April to the 30th of Sept., 1883, inclusive, amounting to $6.50, and that said sum, instead of being paid to the Endowment fund, should be paid into the treasury of each lodge. But this new law was not to take effect unless approved and adopted by a majority of the lodges of this District.

The Grand Secretary duly submitted this proposed law to the lodges, and in his own report for the year ending Dec. 31, 1882, remarked : " It is claimed, and with apparent correctness, that similar benefits can be obtained in other institutions and societies for less money. We have said with APPARENT CORRECTNESS, but we believe that time will show that our plan of endowment is the *safest*, and thereby necessarily the *cheapest* form of co-operative insurance. Its

present cost is caused by the provision in our
law creating and maintaining a sinking fund to
provide against future contingencies. This
sinking fund is the guarantee, and the only one
we have, against an increase of assessments,
which must in time become burdensome unless
a fund of the kind is provided. We do not believe that the sinking fund should be tampered
with, but should be maintained inviolate,
strengthened, secured, and never touched except when needed."

And yet, as shown, the destruction of that
sinking fund was demanded by the lodges. The
proposed new Endowment law, adopted by their
Grand Lodge, after protracted and laborious
meetings, sugar-coated all over with so-called
liberal provisions, aiming "to meet the wishes of
the entire brotherhood," was rejected by the
lodges.[31] This was the result of their being the
custodians of the Endowment fund, instead of
its being kept separate, under the management

---

31. The law was declared rejected on a TIE vote—16
lodges voting for and 16 lodges against the proposed Endowment law. The votes of two lodges were thrown out
on account of informalities. It is noteworthy that JEDID-
JAH and HASMONEA Lodges had voted FOR the law.

of a board of trustees of the Grand Lodge. Yet, results far more serious were to be the issues of that injudicious measure, dictated and fostered by a foolish local pride and a more than foolish distrust. Are Grand Lodges anything else than the chosen members of the lodges ? chosen for their devotion to the Order; brothers who, after years of faithful services in different stations, have proven themselves worthy of the confidence of their brethren.

At its next convention, in Feb., 1884, the Grand Lodge felt it below its dignity to attempt any further amendments to the Endowment law with the exception of prescribing the form of registry, in compliance with the ruling of the U. S. Treasury Department, as follows : " *The trustees of———Lodge, No. ———, I.O.B.B., in trust for the Endowment sinking fund of District Grand Lodge, No. 5, I. O. B. B.*"

In the month of May, 1884, the attention of the general committee was called to the fact that two lodges—Jedidjah, No. 7, and Hasmonea, No. 45—wilfully violated their obligations, and by a vote of a large majority of their members refused to comply with the law (to register the bonds of the Endowment fund "*in trust*" of District

Grand Lodge, No. 5), and it was feared that these funds would be made away with. To prevent this, said two lodges were suspended, injunctions were issued and receivers temporarily appointed. A special meeting of the Grand Lodge was called to consider this grave matter; the same was held in Baltimore, Md., August 19th, 1884, and the charters of Jedidjah, No. 7, and Hasmonea, No. 45, the two oldest and largest lodges of the District, were declared forfeited ; the general committee was empowered to obtain possession of their funds by legal proceedings, and to the loyal members of said two lodges proper protection was secured. These members at once petitioned for a new charter, and in Sept., 1884, two new lodges, Loyal Lodge, No. 350, and Fidelity Lodge, No. 353, new in name, but old in loyal devotion to the Order of B'nai B'rith, arose from the ashes of the two extinct lodges.

Jedidjah Lodge, No. 7, and Hasmonea Lodge, No. 45, appealed against the action of D. G. L., No. 5, to our court of appeals,[32] which court

32. The grounds of appeal, the answer of the District Grand Lodge and the opinions of the court are fully published with the proceedings of the General Convention held

affirmed the action of the District Grand Lodge. The two lodges were lawfully expelled and the appeal dismissed.

At the next following annual convention of

---

in New York, March, 1885, pages 191-234 ; all the judges of our court concur, except only J. Moses, dissenting. He bases his opinion for sustaining the appeal on the ground that the forfeiture in the case at bar was ordered at a SPECIAL MEETING of the Grand Lodge. The law of the Order provides that if any lodge refuse to obey. &c. . . . and if such refusal be persisted in until the meeting of the Grand Lodge next following, said Grand Lodge shall declare the charter of such offending lodge forfeited." A provision for forfeiture will always be strictly construed and the act will be jealously watched as to its legality.

In the circuit court of Baltimore the case was decided in favor of the lodges and that the injunction be dissolved and the receiver discharged. Judge Phelps, of that court, says, in his opinion that : " It is laid down as a rule, absolutely without exception, that equity never lends its aid towards the enforcement of forfeitures and penalties.'' The Judge seems to ignore the fact, or it may not have been clearly presented by the attorneys of the District Grand Lodge, that the Endowment fund is a DISTRICT FUND and never did belong to the lodges; furthermore that his decision works a forfeiture against the loyal members of those lodges. The amounts involved are : Endowment fund in custody of Jedidjah Lodge, $9060.45 ; in the custody of Hasmonea Lodge, $8787.25. The case will now go to the court of appeals.

District Grand Lodge, No. 5, held at Washington, D.C., Feb. 25th, 1885, the firm and dignified action of the President, displayed on occasions that threatened the future weal and existence of the District, received the highest commendation.

And yet, when it came to adopting his recommendations with regard to the Endowment fund, his counsel did not prevail. In his report the President said: "The lesson to be learned from the unfortunate troubles of the two rebellious lodges of Baltimore is, to my mind, the most convincing argument that the most doubting could exact, that *no Endowment* law can be secure unless based upon the requisite of a centralized sinking fund administered by officers directly appointed and controlled by the Grand Lodge. I therefore most earnestly recommend that some measure that will accomplish that idea be at once inaugurated, and the disgraceful proceedings of the past year will, in my judgment, never again be chronicled in the history of the Order. . . . . To your earnest, thoughtful consideration I commend this question as one that involves the permanency, even existence, of the Order. . . . . We must build a wall around the ark of our Endowment fund that will be a perpetual bar in the future to any subordinate lodge, at its pleasure, converting that fund to its own use; and that can only be done by some system of centralization." The committee on Endowment also recommended, with *four* against *one* member, that the fund be centralized. The minority report of *one*, however, claiming that it would involve an expense, if the majority report were adopted, was put upon its passage and adopted. Also a proposition to reduce the contributions from $3.75 to $3.00 per quarter for this year; but the suggestion of the eminent Secretary of the District, that the law be amended " so as to allow the general committee to levy an assessment, sufficient to pay one Endowment, in advance of the actual requirements, thereby avoiding delays, nearly inevitable under existing laws"—was not acted upon at all.

The argument brought forward that "it would involve an expense," may be seen in its true light when we consider that, in District No. 5, under the system of keeping the funds in the care, management and custody of the lodges, it requires thirty-four boards of trustees

and the keeping of its accounts by thirty-four
secretaries ; under the system of centralization
it needs but one board and only the Secretary of
the District, who must after all correspond and
keep those accounts with every lodge. But in
the one case this may be done—but how done !
—without pay ; in the other the District Secretary might probably be allowed a few hundred
dollars of additional compensation. Which is
the proper, cheaper, better method ?

The late Constitution Grand Lodge has decided this point at least.

But there is another, far more important reason for relieving the lodges from the custody
and management of the Endowment fund,
namely, the removal of troublesome money
matters and their discussion from the lodge-
room, whose atmosphere—freed from that heavy
cloud which darkened its light and caused many
a storm—might then become clear, pure, more
attractive to its members. Should they then
fail to make it so, fail to cultivate the higher
aims and objects of the Order, the reason could
no longer be designated by—"all on account of
Endowment."

Let us now look at DISTRICT No. 6. The progressive character of our Order in this District is an established fact ; the best representatives of modern enlightened Judaism may be found in its ranks. It possesses a phalanx of brethren who are serving the advancement of the Order with ability, fidelity and unremitting zeal. Nevertheless, as shown in the former part of this study (pages 48-58), this District was unsuccessful in its attempts to adopt a sound plan; but there is no bitter feeling about it ; their Trustees of the Endowment Reserve Fund wisely said : " Like all other human devices, our system of endowment has its imperfections, but the benefits, so far, overshadow these, that we can afford to ignore them."

Thus, for years, the endowment was carried on, under the fifty cents assessment plan, producing a small surplus at each case of death. This surplus gradually increasing from $100 to about $270, as the membership and the number of deaths increased, was erroneously deemed " sufficient to satisfy the wishes of our most ardent supporters of a large reserve fund."

Had the membership continued to increase in the same ratio as it had up to 1882, this rate of assessments would gradually have reached, and even exceeded, $15 per annum ; and investing its accumulation at seven per cent. interest, as its trustees did, it would finally have produced the necessary reserve ; but, as their President correctly remarked in his message to this District Grand Lodge meeting at Peoria, in Jan., 1882: "Already the history of the last few years shows us that the time for a rapid increase of membership is gone ; the attractions offered by the Order have been in existence long enough to have induced all those to join who have passed the first meridian of manhood, and, generally speaking, our recruits are now from the young men, and are not more than enough to keep our membership numerically about the same."

But the death-rate cannot remain the same—

In 1876 . . . 9 members died.
" 1877 . . 9 " "
" 1878 . . 10 " "
" 1879 . . . 18 " "
" 1880 . . 17 " "
" 1881 . . . 22 " "
" 1882 . . . 28 " "

And the President, directing attention to the

fact that it must largely increase in future time, said: "The 2500 members in the District are all bound to die during the next forty years, making an average of over sixty a year . . . and that man must be blind who cannot see that, at some future time, the yearly death-rates will be as much above sixty as they hitherto have been below. But long before that time shall have come, our endowment system, unless put on some enduring basis, will have gone to wreck and ruin, and drawn our Order with it into one common gulf of destruction. . . . The only remedy against these terrible consequences lies in the establishment of a rapidly increasing sinking fund. It should have been established long ago."

But, through 1882, the system remained unchanged. Every motion to amend the Endowment law, was objected to as inadmissible under the laws of this District, which required a petition of two-thirds of its lodges before any proposition changing sections 1 and 2 of their endowment law could be entertained by the Grand Lodge. The President, an eminent jurist, doubted the validity of a law depriving the Grand Lodge of the power to legislate, and the restriction was finally repealed ; nevertheless, the same Grand Lodge decided, by a vote of 35 against 23, that at this convention the rate of assessment (50 cents at every death) remain undisturbed.

Already at the next Grand Lodge Convention, however, a new endowment law was enacted, which provided for fixed endowment dues of $15 annually, payable in quarterly instalments of $3.75. The Grand Secretary's report to that session showed that, under the system of 50 cents assessments *without limit*,[33] an emergency may arise, at any moment, compelling the secretary to make assessment for an extraordinary number of deaths, in consequence of which many members, especially the younger ones, would withdraw, and the influx of new members

---

33. The system of 50 *cents assessments* WITHOUT LIMITS is theoretically quite sound for a membership exceeding two thousand, as it will produce over $1000 as long as that membership does not decrease ; and the surplus accumulated while the number of members is above 2000, would probably cover the deficit when it falls below that number ; but the assessments must, sooner or later, become very burdensome, and consequently this system is impracticable.

would be stopped for ever. In fact he already had to make a levy for five deaths in the month of July of that year, and members were about to withdraw in great numbers, so that—but for the promise of changing the law and limiting the contribution at the next Grand Lodge session, a stampede would have been the result. And thus it came that in January, 1883, the long-desired, oft-defeated system (similar to the one of District No. 2) was adopted, by a vote of 58 to 4: *"all delegates voting in the affirmative except Bros. Geo. Braham, Max Stern, Isaac Weil and D. W. Simon."*

But, shortly after the adjournment, a few dis-satisfied members distributed a "remonstrance"[34]

---

34. This Remonstrance was a mere reiteration of the sufficiently controverted *opinion* that "one generation should not be made to hoard a large capital for future generations;" that " the sinking fund, however large this sum may be in the annual report, may eventually prove to be so only on paper;" that "the law is injurious to the interest of the Lodges of the District, &c.;" that "it was hastily (!) passed, without due notice and proper consideration " and "should be immediately repealed," for which purpose a special meeting of District Grand Lodge, No. 6, should be called. For all of these statements the remonstrance offered neither proof nor argument. It merely stated that "it would be

demanded a call for a SPECIAL SESSION, and
finally agreed that the constitutionality of the
new law be tested by an appeal to the court of
appeals. Two prominent members—a rabbi and
a lawyer—championed the appeal. The rabbi
admitted "that the purest motives actuated the
enthusiastic advocates of that law," and "that
only an enormous reserve fund could secure the
permanency of our endowments;" but he

---

best to subdivide the Endowment Reserve Fund, *pro rata*,
to the lodges, and have every lodge keep its own fund,
subject to the disposition of the Grand Lodge. Thereby the
fund would always be secure and safe. *Vide* District No.
5 ! and also District No. 7, whose President said in his
message, delivered in May, 1885: "The only argument in
favor of allowing the fund to remain in the hands of the
different lodges, is the one of safety against defalcation.
On the other hand, experience has demonstrated that
where the fund is divided into a number of smaller ones,
a large proportion thereof necessarily remains idle and the
balance is not invested to best advantage. The income
from the fund will be largely increased and its safety
guaranteed, if the whole fund be consolidated and placed
under the management of a Board of Trustees. Our experience at Vicksburg, with the fund of Enrogel Lodge,
must convince the most skeptical, that even under our
present system (said lodge holding its own share of the
fund), we are not safe against loss."

thought that it was not legally enacted ; that it was in conflict with the laws of the State of Illinois—as he had been told by his brother the lawyer. The latter gentleman tried to make the members believe that the mere change from *post mortem* assessments to quarterly dues, would subject us to all the burdens imposed upon regular Life Insurance Companies, that it would cause the Attorney-General of the State of Illinois to file information against the District, and that the penalties provided for by statutes as punishment for those who prosecute the *business of life insurance* UNLAWFULLY would be incurred. Nobody knew better than that very lawyer, that there was not the least danger of any such result. The statute of Illinois, herein referred to, was adopted *in favor of corporations* NOT *for pecuniary profit,* and at the request of benevolent organizations intended to benefit the widows, orphans and devisees of their members; the law was intended for our protection; and no attorney-General would ever have instituted *quo warranto* proceedings, on the ground that our society might quarterly collect a stipulated amount.

The framers of said statute considered *assess-*

ments as *one* of the features that distinguished benevolent societies from regular life insurance companies collecting annual premiums.

To remove this mere shadow and at the same time comply in form with the State law, the General Committee expressly empowered by the Grand Lodge "to properly frame that Endowment law" and "see to the correct phraseology thereof"—changed the wording of Section 2 accordingly; but this by no means satisfied the appellants. And the appeal was sustained; not however because of a conflict with the State law, but simply for the omission of a formality; the NAMES of those voting *for it* were not recorded; three judges only concurring,[35] three not voting, and one dissenting!—With the exception of two, all lodges of the District had paid the first quarter, notwithstanding the fact that the appeal was then pending.

This decision, however, annulled the new law and the District had to be governed by the old one. Had the new Endowment law been main-

35 It was rumored that the vote was 2 for and 2 against the appeal—and that the judge from District No. 6, who favored the appellants, finally succeeded in bringing one judge over to his side.

tained the increase of the Reserve fund would have been more than double the amount for that year. The Trustees say in their report that in their opinion that the decision arrived at by the court was "prompted by a mistaken generosity," that the anxiety felt about the safety of the Reserve fund was groundless and had given way to more rational reasoning.

Irreparable injury was done by that appeal and its decision;—a by far greater harm, a far more deplorable injury than the loss of a few thousand dollars of the Reserve fund. The District was in a vortex of excitement, if not strife. The General Committee itself was divided on this endowment question, and though the executive officers tried to steer the ship safely through the tempest aroused by the struggle, there was a decline in membership and the District had made a step backward. A larger number of members than ever before allowed themselves to be suspended for non–payment of dues while the dues were *less* than in the preceding year. Hence it was quite natural that the President who had most zeal·ously labored to promote the welfare of the institution he so dearly loved, felt discouraged.

In his message to the Grand Lodge meeting, held at Chicago in January, 1884, he attributes the situation to "the unwholesomeness of the appeal and the dissensions in the General Committee." He says:

"It is to be regretted that the Honorable Court seemingly evaded the rendering of a decision upon the vital points at issue, and apparently resorted to finding a technical flaw. This must have been as disappointing to the appellants as to every other member who had interested himself in the case, especially to those fifty-eight of the sixty-two members attending our last year's session, who were happy in the thought of having placed our District on firmer footing than it had ever been.

"That the Law had worked satisfactorily to all, excepting probably to a small fraction, was shown by the prompt payment of nearly all amounts due to the Endowment Fund.

"Aside of the mischief done by reason of the appeal to the progress of the Lodges, the Reserve Fund is minus about $12,000, which if in the treasury, would be at least one important factor in contributing to the stability of our institution. Our members became accustomed to the systematic payment of their dues. The majority of Lodges that had not already adopted the regular installment plan in previous times, found its workings now admirable for the convenience of members and the collection of outstandings, and I can say with the fullest assurance, that had this fire-brand not been thrust into the plans and work of the present administration, I would be enabled to lay before you better results of our labors than I do."

After referring to the breach in the General Committee, eventuating in continuous differ-ences of opinion on nearly all issues and in threats of asking the courts to issue an injunc-tion, he continues thus:

"It may be justifiable from a legal standpoint, to clog the wheels of a benevolent institution; it may also be allowable to discuss in public places, highways or halls, the justness of laws and measures, but the motives of issuing inflammatory circulars, threaten-ing prosecution, arousing animosities and the like action must certainly be regarded somewhat inconsis-tent with those requisites, which should form part of men's good intention in an order like ours, especially as impelling them to protect and assist widows and orphans. It was only through the wise councils of some of our most distingished members that these contaminating influences were checked."

And in his melancholy mood, while memory watched o'er the sad review of the past year, he tried to consider some of the causes of the de-cline and the possible remedies. The former appear to him to centre in the Endowment question. He thinks that before its insidious entrance in our organization . . . . few if any of our old members joined the Order B'nai B'rith with the expectation of reaping any benefit in a material sense; he supposed that the beneficence to the needy widow and orphan directly bestowed by the Lodges was far in excess to the present advantages, derived from the $1,000 Endowment benefit; he saw in the shadowy past the Lodge meetings well and regularly attended and suspensions scarcely known.

The order of things has greatly changed,—he remarks.—The man who does not want his life insured is excluded from membership; thus many worthy men, men with no selfish purpose in view, are kept out and many would not join us because of the compulsory law, who would do so if this feature were not enforced.

The president then proceeds to consider the remedies; and he recommends, *first* the enactment of laws, "making it *optional* with members and applicants to remain or become endowment members," and he supports this recommendation with warm eloquence.

I have dwelt at such length on this president's

message because it is the first official document of that kind which has given impetus to this rather popular demand for *an optional endowment*, and its author is certainly entitled to highest regard, both for ability and purity of motives.

But is it true that many would join if the Endowment feature were optional? By no means! Would the former method of each Lodge, giving a small stipend to the widows and orphans of its deceased members, be more satisfactory and become less oppressive? Certainly not. Those who have "worked and watched" for our Order, those, who, like myself, have long opposed the introduction of assessment-insurance to our brotherhood, know that the demand *for* it was general and irresistible; know that the failure to introduce it in District No. 2, caused the separation of the Southern Lodges, forming District No. 7; know that kindred Jewish organizations owe their rise to the demand for endowment. Many would not join us of late—not because they do not want insurance, but because they can get it for less in other societies, and some withdrew for the same reason. O, yes, if endowment could be made optional, with the privilege of joining thereafter, at any time, discontinuing and rejoining at pleasure, this would be considered very nice. But it *cannot* be done under a system of uniform contributions, and *should not* be allowed under any system *in fraternal organizations*. In District No. 7 the endowment has lately been made optional to young men until they reach the age of thirty. My proposed Endowment law submitted to the late Constitution Grand Lodge by the Executive Committee, recommended making it optional for young, unmarried, up to age of thirty-five. This is the utmost extent to which *optional* endowment might be permitted. As soon as a brother gets married and assumes the responsibility of providing for his family—it becomes his duty to insure the same against misery and want in case of his demise. And if some brethren, while enjoying health and strength, forget that

"Death still draws nearer, never seeming near;"
if others, blessed with ample means and flattering prospects, forget that

"Riches take unto themselves wings;"
if some fool pretends to be sure of the distant future, to need no protection, and not to care for the welfare of "future generations"—

"Yet ne'er looks farther than his nose;"
then *"Let the wise make the rest obey."*

The committee on endowment of that District Grand Lodge (Jan., 1884) endorsed the recommendation of the President to make the endowment *optional;* yet it did not prevail; nor did the proposition to charge 75 cents at each assessment limiting these to twenty per year, as was proposed in a new Endowment law, prepared by the General Committee. Said law was adopted after a long and hot discussion, amended, however, to unlimited assessments at 50 cts.; thus virtually remaining the same as before.

At the end of another year, (January, 1885), the President of District Grand Lodge No. 6, reported that "the dissatisfactions and controversies of the preceding year regarding the Endowment proved to be a thing of the past under the present law, and peace and harmony prevailed . . . It will remain so until the number of deaths will exceed the expectations of those who desire to legislate only for to-day without any regard of what will come to-morrow, and then it will be discovered that the turmoil of last year is only 'aufgeschoben—nicht aufgehoben,' and will again break forth with greater force and energy than before." . . . .

"*I hope that the Constitution Grand Lodge will be able to solve this problem.*" He also favored "OPTIONAL ENDOWMENT," but says: "Were it not for the vested rights of those who have joined our Order, partly induced thereto by this very Endowment, I would hail with joy the day on which the entire Endowment would be abolished."

But the majority of the members will not consent to its abolishment. The eminent Trustees of the Endowment Fund of District No. 6, said in their last report: "The Endowments paid have proven very beneficial in most cases, and in many instances the only source of revenue and sustenance left to its recipients, thereby not only alleviating misery but furnishing the means for self-support. Let us earnestly hope and strive that we may always be able to give substantial aid; that our system of Endowment be placed upon a basis of permanency, furnishing lasting benefits to those who receive them and happiness to us who sustain this noble monument of our Order."

DISTRICT No. 6, with its young vigorous membership, its salubrious climate, with ample

material for numerical increase, with a reserve
fund of over $60,000, and further accumula-
tion, invested at over six per·cent. interest;
this District will be able to protect all its members' widows and orphans at the rate of $15 per
annum. And though, in later years, the advance
in age and decline in the rate of interest may
make a slight increase of the annual assessments
necessary—say to $18—then, when the many
bubbles of cheap insurance will have burst,
this will be readily assented to by the very members who have heretofore objected to $15.
Moreover, this amount would soon be exceeded
at the present rate of 50 cents on every death.
I cannot doubt, therefore, that the next Grand
Lodge will already place the Endowment fund
of District No. 6, on a sound and enduring
basis; and that the long struggles and ordeals
she has passed through will be spared to her
future sessions. I hope that those who think
that most of our members have joined the Order
induced by the Endowment, and at the same
time believe it is the Endowment that keeps
many men from joining us—will recognize the
self·contradiction of these two assertions.
There are, no doubt, some men who were partly

attracted by the natural desire to secure protection for those dearest to them in life—when they themselves will be called hence, there may be a few others who are kept from us by the insurance feature, and many more by being offered greater benefits for less money in other societies. It must be our aim to do right; not to please all.

Let those who seek only the sham of cheap insurance—stay out; let those who joined our Order for no other purpose—withdraw in peace.

DISTRICT No. 7, has been the subject of this study in the first pages of this long, sad chapter (Part III). The opinion therein expressed as to the grave errors of its Endowment laws—which the late Grand Secretary considered "as perfect as human heads could frame them,"—has lately been endorsed by the President of that District, who said in his address to the Grand Lodge (May 1885), "The plan formulated and adopted at the Galveston Convention in 1882, depends for its success upon a steady revenue of at least four per cent upon our reserve, and an annual increase of our membership of not less than one per cent. Anything less than these conditions renders an Endowment system unsafe." But their reserve fund, instead of increasing and accumulating at interest—decreases. On Dec. 31st, 1884, it was $5,851 less than on the year previous; it now amounts to less than $12,000. There is, besides, a District Endowment fund held by the various (62) lodges. The amount of this fund cannot be ascertained from the last G. L. report. In the President's address to the preceding G. L. meeting (1884), it was stated that: "the large proportion of the whole fund is uninvested, said to be 'in currency,' and bearing no interest; some of the lodges carry their whole fund in this shape. The message of my honored predecessor recommended, and the Dallas Convention ordered, that all such sums should be invested, but no attention has been paid to this. I venture the assertion that this currency is not laid up in stockings or safe drawers, nor deposited in bank to the credit of this particular fund; and lodges who allow the trustees to use it, should be made to pay the interest, which, by their neglect of duty, the District fails to obtain." The entire financial condition of the funds for this District is in confusion.

In January 1879, *after* the epidemic, the

membership of District No. 7, was 2665, since then it has annually decreased, until in January 1884, it was reduced to 2318. There is no complete report for the year 1884, owing to the sickness and subsequent death of the Secretary

And in the face of these undeniable facts, the members of the Executive Committee for the District, in February 1885, reported that "they regard their own Endowment as near perfection as can be reached." Comment is unnecessary.

This condition of the Endowment in our various Districts—threatening the peace and harmony, assailing the honor and integrity of the Order,—besides other questions affecting the welfare of our brotherhood,—prompted our M. W. President, Bro. Julius Bien, to call a meeting of the Executive Committee. He said: "unless the evil is speedily checked, I fear that disturbances and disruptions may follow, which it would be too late to heal. I have repeatedly called attention to the seriousness of this question, and to the inevitable consequences involved in a disregard of the true principles underlying a safe and secure Endowment law; but my warnings have not been heeded. I see no other way out of the present dilemma, in the absence of any other authority, than through the action of a General Convention, where the representative men of the Order, in their united wisdom, will determine upon the means and measures necessary to prevent the Order from being diverted from its true course, and give a fresh impulse to its higher and nobler aspirations."

The Executive Committee met and resolved that the lodges be communicated with for that purpose. In conformity with this resolution, the lodges were called upon to express their opinion for or against a special Convention; and in that call the Executive Committee stated as one of the reasons which had actuated them to take this step, the following:

"The Widow and Orphan Endowment having caused so great an agitation in most of the Districts as to overshadow nearly every other object of the Order, threatens to seriously interfere with its progress and prosperity.

The Endowment law has been declared to be *within the scope of the Order* by our last Convention; it therefore behooves the Order to *spread such safeguards around it* as to advance rather than to jeopardize the welfare of our Districts and Lodges, and to *assign to it its proper position* in our benevolent aspiration."

A large majority of the lodges voted in favor of holding the proposed special meeting of the Constitution Grand Lodge. The solution of the Endowment question was generally considered to be its engrossing topic. The supreme legislature of the Order met at Tammany Hall, New York, on March 1st, 1885, about two hundred delegates attending. The message of the President of the Executive Committee set forth the fact that there were also other potent topics demanding serious attention and consideration. This admirable paper, which should be studied by every brother, says with reference to the spirit then prevailing in the Order:

"There is a deeply felt want, a want of genuine unity and true fraternal concord amongst our Districts.

There seems to be a lack of some tangible object which would create closer relations and call into action the Order as an entirety.

Material interests, which of late have taken an un-

due prominence, may safely be left in the care of the
Districts; they offer no common rallying point; on the
contrary, some of these material interests, as will be
shown, have rather a tendency to disturb the harmony of our Order and to imperil its welfare.

The old flame of enthusiasm must be rekindled if
we mean to arrest the growing indifferentism; the
higher principles must again be brought to the fore-
ground; the life-giving spirit must be evoked to re-
establish the solidarity of the Order, from which we
are drifting away.

Without it we have no future."

With reference to the Widow and Orphan
Endowment the words of that message are as
follows:

"One of the principal objects of the Order from its
inception was the care and support of the Widows
and Orphans of deceased brethren.

The provisions made for them in the early days
were rather scant, but conformed to the modest
demands of the time.

With the growth of the Order, the changed condition and requirements of life, as well as the natural
increase in the number of deaths from year to year,
the revenue derived from the small Widow and Orphan funds of the Lodges proved insufficient, and it
became evident that a change in the existing method
was necessary.

After extended discussions of various propositions
made by committees appointed for the purpose,
District Grand Lodge No. 1 adopted an amendment
to its by-laws, whereby each member of the District
(then numbering over 4,000) contributed twenty-five
cents at the death of a brother, and the sum of $1,000
was paid to the Widow and Orphans. This was the
beginning of our present Endowment system.

In time all the other Districts, from the same necessity, adopted the Endowment plan, variously formulated into laws, which were changed and altered as
occasion demanded, or ill-advised reduction of assessments prompted. An attempt, made at the Convention of 1874 in Chicago, to consolidate the interests of
all the Districts into a General Endowment for the
whole Order, failed, but the declaration was made,
'That the establishment of Widows' and Orphans'
Endowment Funds is within the legitimate scope of
the aims and objects of the Order.'

Doubts soon arose as to the permanency of the
institution on the plan pursued, and wholesome and
sound advice was not wanting. It remained unheeded, however, because of a general disinclination to
consider future needs, largely engendered by a clamor
for cheap insurance, and a want of comprehension of
the principles involved.

The progressive death rate brought with it additional taxation, which threatened to become oppressive,

and beyond the means of many brethren, if not checked by remedial legislation.

District No. 2 alone adopted a law insuring the permanency of its endowment.

District No. 7 unwisely increasing its endowment to $1,000, surrounded its law with some safeguards.

District No. 1, in the face of strenuous and continued opposition, has still accumulated a reserve fund, which as yet is by no means sufficient, but all the attempts of the better informed and well-meaning brethren have failed to make adequate provision for the future,

Districts Nos. 4, 5 and 6, the first with an Endowment of $2,000, have repeatedly changed their laws, and with some improvement, but by no means meeting the requirements of the case ; while Districts No. 3, has made no provision whatever for future demands that will assuredly be made.

It is fifteen years since the endowment law was passed in District No. 1, and a crisis is approaching in this, as in other Districts.

A feeling of uncertainty, of lurking danger, has become widespread; fallacies, which appeal powerfully to the ignorant and mercenary, such as to perpetuate an average age by the accession of new members, and to profit by it in obtaining a large life insurance by small payments, have at last been generally dissipated, but without changing the fatal course, leading inevitably to disaster.

To aggravate the situation, many of our brethren have affiliated with other Jewish societies offering endowment benefits similar to our own, and for no other apparent purpose than to secure a larger amount of cheap life insurance.

The burden thereby assumed has proven too heavy for many, hence the outcry against onerous taxation and the constantly swelling list of suspensions for non-payment of dues.

An agitation detrimental to every other interest has consequently been kept up for several years. In Grand Lodge meetings the endowment is the predominant, all-absorbing subject of interminable, passionate and profitless discussion. Lodges have taken a threatening attitude, and complications arising out of this question have already led to the expulsion of two of the older Lodges from the Order. A solution of this problem must be speedily arrived at, as it is evident that a continuance of the present state of affairs will defeat the benevolent object sought to be attained, bankrupt existing endowment funds and carry in its wake want and distress to many homes, as well as destruction to a portion, if not to the whole Order.

Widows' and Orphans' endowment funds have been sanctioned by the Constitution Grand Lodge; it becomes now its solemn and imperative duty to avert the dangers which have arisen from their establishment.

The endowment feature must either be entirely eliminated from the Order, relegating to the Lodges the support of their widows and orphans, as their means will permit, or a District Widow and Orphan Endowment law, permanent in its character, honest, just and equitable, must be engrafted on our Constitution.

Such a law should be based on principles tersely stated by Brother Bush :

1. Man is mortal, and the inevitable decline of life cannot be neutralized by adding more lives.

2. To pay out a certain sum at the death of every member, the aggregate amount must also be paid by the members.

3. As some men die before they can have paid as much as their beneficiaries receive, others must make good that deficiency.

4. This deficiency must be made good by paying in the early years a sum sufficient to accumulate a reserve which, increased by interest, will balance the deficiency.

" Such a law has been prepared by Brother Bush. . . . . . It is presented to you with my earnest endorsement. Its adoption will ensure for all future time the incalculable benefits, of which the past has furnished a brilliant example, it will open the doors of our Lodges to men at the best time of life, who have, until now, been excluded by the limitation of age, and by ending a hurtful agitation, give way to a calm pursuit of our intellectual and ethical aspirations, and

attract to our ranks the young men of Israel, who are
our hope and reliance for the perpetuation of our
beloved Order.[1]

Against his desire the writer was appointed

——·

[1]. This proposed Endowment law is published as Ap-
pendix No. 3 to the "Proceedings of the General Convention of the I.O.B.B., held in New York, March 1-6, 1885,"
pages 237-245.

Before proceeding any further, the originator of that law
wishes to state that he has been materially aided in framing
the same by some of the ablest brothers of the Order.   It
was one of the chief aims of the framers of the law to make
it as satisfactory to all reasonable demands as was possible
without sacrificing any fundamental principle of justice and
safety; and yet under that unwise and unjust system of
representation—now fortunately abolished—its acceptance
by a two-thirds majority of the delegates elected, was
doubtful.   This doubt grew as propositions from different
lodges and members were presented.   Some asked for a
consolidation of all Districts under ONE general Endowment
law; others protested against any and every interference
with their District Endowment.

The author of this Study has not thought of proposing a
consolidated Endowment fund.   For, however wise and
beneficial such a plan would have been, if adopted in 1874,
the condition of the District Endowment funds of that time
differs so widely from that of the present Endowment funds,
and these differ so widely from each other, as to make it
altogether impracticable.

Chairman of the Committee on Endowment.
This committee consisted of eleven members
from the various Districts, and held protracted
sessions. Though unanimous in cordially en-
dorsing and recommending the proposed law—
yet the eighteen dollar clause was strongly objected to ; it being held by some that in their
Districts the annual contribution need not be
more than fifteen dollars. In vain was it represented to them that the great desideratum was a
UNIFORM rate and a complete law which would
free the Grand Lodges from all further discussions and dissensions concerning Endowment
legislation; that $18 was certainly safer; that in
case of a continuance of favorable conditions of
mortality and interest in any District, its Grand
Lodge would, in later years, be enabled to entirely exempt its members—after reaching the
age of seventy five—from paying any assessments; a feature much to be desired, but impossible of accomplishment at less than $18. In
vain were these and other arguments used ; the
majority of the committee declared itself ready
to sign a report in favor of adopting the law as
recommended by the President of the Executive Committee, *provided* the rate be changed to

"NOT LESS THAN $15 ANNUALLY." The delegates of District No. 6 sent assurances to the committee that, if so amended, the proposed law would receive their almost unanimous vote, but not otherwise. Several members of the committee would not decide whether or not to sign such report, until submitted to them in writing. Hence the chairman felt himself INSTRUCTED to report as follows :

"We fully recognize the fact that, with advancing age and the inevitable increase of mortality, the endowment system would become very burdensome and end in disastrous failure, unless it were placed on a sound and enduring basis.

"Attempts to improve the prevailing system and provide for the necessary reserve funds have absorbed the time and attention of most of our Grand Lodge sessions, without satisfactory results and to the great detriment of the progress of our lodges.

" The experience of the last decade has fully demonstrated the fact that there is no hope of obtaining a correct, sound and enduring endowment system through District legislation before it would be too late. Some may think that it would be of no great consequence were the endowment system to fail, arguing that the Endowment Fund is not the Order B'nai B'rith; and that, having existed, grown and flourished without endowments, it could again exist without them.

"Certainly it could had they never been introduced; but, having been introduced, and being at present a part of our Order, we deem it incumbent upon us to make our endowment system an honest and permanent one. Were we to maintain a delusion, making it impossible to keep faith with our brethren; were we to permit and sustain a deception, it would become disastrous to a great number of our members, a disgrace to our Order, and consequently its ruin.

" The undersigned members of your committee, therefore, have arrived at the conclusion that it is the duty of this Constitution Grand Lodge, and would be to the best interest of our fraternity, to pass a law which shall be binding on those Districts of our Order that intend to carry on and maintain an Endowment Fund.

" Should the members of any District prefer to persevere in its present scheme, those members might form a separate organization under whatever name and jurisdiction they please, but such organization should certainly not be allowed to bear the honored name of the Independent Order B'nai B'rith, nor to form an integral part of our Order.

" The law which we submit for your consideration and adoption is, with some few modifications, the one prepared by the Chairman of this Committee, and commended to you by the President of the Executive Comittee in his message to this Comvention.

" It is *not* a plan for *one* General Endowment Fund, but merely a safe guide for every District 'desiring to carry on and maintain an Endowment Fund,' in conducting it on a sound and enduring basis; it is a system, not merely theoretically correct, but which has been tried and has proved eminently successful in District No. 2.

" It has, besides, some new, liberal and beneficial features, which would prove of value."

The only material change made was, to strike out $18, and insert in lieu thereof the words, " not less than fifteen dollars ($15) annually for each participating member;" and the report expressly states that :

"While the Chairman of the Committee may be fully justified in proposing $18 annually, as the lowest amount required in some Districts for the safety and perpetuity of the Endowment—we believe that in Districts with a younger membership, and where the investment of funds at a higher rate of interest than five per cent. can safely be made, the annual contribution need not be more than $15, at least for the present."

This report was signed by six members of the committee—the others signed a MINORITY RE-

PORT, which "cordially endorsed the plan submitted by Bro. Bush as a wise, efficient and satisfactory scheme of Endowment for the Districts; but, in view of the local statutes of several States of the Union, the difficulty of avoiding any infringement of contract rights, and the legal complications that must necessarily arise in the attempt to enforce a law—obligatory upon District Grand Lodges adopting the endowment feature—it would be inexpedient and impracticable to recommend, at this session, the passage of a system of endowment operating alike upon all the Districts."

The reports were considered together, and a very animated discussion ensued.

Bro. Simon M. ROEDER of New York, Vice-President of the Convention, from District No. 1, made an eloquent speech against both reports; appealing to the Convention not to send the delegates home without settling this burning question. He believed that, for District No. 1, the rate required would be no less than twenty dollars; but, relying on the expert knowledge of Bro. Bush, would have been satisfied with eighteen dollars. The members of his District were NOW paying very nearly fifteen dollars and —under its present system of paying 14 cents *per capita* for each death up to one and a half per cent of its membership—their annual contribution would soon reach or even exceed $18; but by adopting a law which sanctions a rate of $15, every advance would be obstructed. The young men, though willing to pay more, in order to lighten the burden of their elder brethren, were not willing to pay for the benefit of those only who might die during the next score years, after which nothing would be left for their own protection.

Bro. J. HIRSCH, of Vicksburg, author of the minority report, made flattering comments about the proposed law—but, at some length and with great force, presented the legal difficulties. In his District (No. 7), especially where an Endowment of $1500 was guaranteed, the reduction of the benefit to $1000 would be looked upon as a violation of the sacred character of funds accumulated under that promise. In his Grand Lodge he would use his best efforts towards securing, in a legal and peaceful manner, the adoption of an Endowment law, similar to the one proposed.

There was much noise and confusion in the Hall, and it was often impossible to hear what was being said. Some speakers seemed to censure the chairman of the committee for having abandoned his position, in reporting contrary to his own opinion. But, as a reply, he referred, in his address to the Convention, to the report wherein he had distinctly stated that the members of the committee had INSTRUCTED him thus to report. He said: "If it were your intention to erect a building, strong and enduring, you would not devote yourself to the study of architecture and engineering, you would not ask your physician, your banker, or your tailor, as to how you should proceed;—you would consult an expert architect, who knew what you wanted; you would let him make the plans and estimate the cost. You now wish to erect a tower of protection, an institution that shall stand for centuries to come, shall brave all storms and be equal to all emergencies, not only for a certain number of years, but for ever. Your will may determine what kind of protection you wish to insure, for what amount you wish to provide; but you cannot say you will do so with so many cents of assessments, or so many dollars a year.

The plan for the foundation and construction as well as the computation of its cost must be made by the scientific expert. Being possessed of some knowledge on this subject—the result of many years of study and experience—I have made the plans, estimated the cost, and after careful consideration, due examination, and consulting with other experts, I have submitted the plan and cost for your investigation and action. Your committee endorse the plan with rare unanimity, but believe that in some localities the cost will be a little less than in others. This may be. It is the duty of the chairman to report as the committee have instructed him. It is for the *collective wisdom* of this Convention to decide what it deems best."

Thereupon Bro. Simon Wolf, of Washington, D.C., presented the following substitute for both reports.[2]

---

2. Bro. S. Wolf offered his substitute verbally only. The secretary, Bro. Alfred T. Jones, wrote it down, and both kindly submitted it to the chairman of the committee for correction. This correction was made hastily—many members pressing for a recess— and an imperfect wording was the result. But it was wisely ordained by the Convention (Proceedings page 157) that the Executive Committee

WIDOW AND ORPHAN ENDOWMENT LAW.

Sect. 1. The creation or maintenance of any endowment system by a District Grand Lodge shall be left entirely to the option of such Grand Lodge.

Sect. 2. If any District Grand Lodge shall decide to enact a law providing for the establishment of an endowment system, or has enacted such law and desires to maintain the same, then in such case the annual assessment shall be fixed at a rate of not less than *fifteen* dollars for every one thousand dollars guaranteed, or in the same proportion for a fractional part thereof.

Sect. 3. Any fund that may be created under the provision contained in sect. 2, shall be under the absolute control of the District Grand Lodge, and not of the individual lodges.

Sect. 4. This law shall go into effect April 1st, 1886.

A motion to amend by inserting "sixteen" in place of fifteen, and a further amendment offered to substitute "eighteen" in place of fifteen or sixteen, were both rejected.

---

have power to make verbal and grammatical changes not affecting the sense. The substitute was offered, intended and clearly understood by all members present as quoted above; and the original wording does not admit of a different sense—any attempted interpretation to the contrary notwithstanding.

This proves that it would have been worse than useless to present a report in favor of the proposed endowment law, *without the change* asked by the committee.

The previous question being ordered, the substitute proposed by Bro. S. Wolf was voted upon. There were 109 votes in the affirmative and only 48 in the negative; it was therefore declared duly enacted as part of our Organic Law.

Bro. Thalmessinger then offered the following resolution, which was adopted without dissent :

"*Resolved*, That aside from the Widow and Orphan Endowment Law just passed by this Convention, the plan submitted to the Convention by Bro. Isidor Bush on that subject is earnestly recommended to the consideration of the Lodges and District Grand Lodges, as representing a valuable guide to those who desire to see the endowment fund firmly established."

The brief law adopted by the Convention enforces the same fundamental rules as are contained in the proposed law, *as submitted by the committee.* By changing the originally proposed endowment law, especially as to the tax, from " eighteen dollars " to " not less than fifteen dollars," the main point of contention, THE RATE, would have been left undetermined, and the object intended by the framer of that law— the uniformity of the endowment and the removal of this subject from the forum of the District Grand Lodges—could not have been attained; it seemed preferable, therefore, that the organic law should simply establish the basis on which the Endowment system must be reorganized in each District, or else discontinued. In promulgating the Constitution of the I. O. B. B., as revised and amended by the Convention, the circular of the Executive Committee of April 25th, 1885, contains the following words in reference to THE WIDOW AND ORPHAN ENDOWMENT LAW:

"It is just and right, that such a benevolent provision should be surrounded with the proper safeguards, to secure an honest and certain fulfilment of our promises, and in this view the Convention has disposed of the vexed question.

"It is left optional with the District to have an Endowment Law or not nor has the amount to be provided for been limited. But a minimum annual contribution has been fixed upon below which no Endowment law can be safely carried out, nor will hereafter be permitted to exist in the Order. Wherever this minimum should be found insufficient, it is left to the respective District to make a proper adjustment adapted to its condition.

"It is earnestly hoped and strongly recommended that all Districts will *at once* loyally harmonize their Endowment Laws with the Constitutional Enactment, and wisely and calmly adopt such measures as will make them safe and permanent, and thereby forever remove an element of disturbance and discord."

Whether or not this will be accomplished, whether wise counsel will prevail and measures be adopted securing the much desired end; or whether the struggles of the past will have been in vain,—the hopes for a harmonious adoption of safe and enduring endowment laws by our District Grand Lodges be again disappointed, —the near future will show.[3]

A study of the history of our Endowments, from their inception to the present day, must surely aid in a correct solution of this problem. Even three hundred years ago, Sir Walter Raleigh already said: "we may gather out of

3. A few of the members, plotting the disruption of the Order, may attempt to deny the right of the Constitution Grand Lodge to legislate on our Endowment, forgetting that the Constitution Grand Lodge is supreme, and they have sworn to obey its laws.

history a policy no less wise than eternal; by the comparison and application of other men's fore-passed miseries with our own like errors." And Carlyle, the great historian of this century says: "History is Philosophy teaching by experience." Very few legislators, however, study history; and popular *delusions, distrusts* and *prejudices*, long and deeply rooted in their minds, will again have to be fought.

(1). DELUSIONS about *"cheap insurance,"* opposing a large reserve as unnecessary, have been amply controverted in the course of this study. If smaller amounts were paid in the beginning, much larger amounts would have to be paid in future years, when the members would have become of a more advanced age and finally the tax would become too burden-some to bear. No assessment insurance, with-out large reserve fund, can practically extend beyond the age of 60 or 65 years.⁴ There is,

---

4. At the age of 65 the mortality (American Table) is 40 in 1000, increasing with each year until at the age of 70 it is 62 out of 1000; at 75 years it is about 95 deaths in 1000; hence the annual net cost of risk must be just as many dollars for one thousand dollars. Add to this the Insur-ance Companies' charge for expenses of management,

no *hocus pocus* in existence, whereby men can receive more than they contribute, except by an accumulation of interest. Those who promise larger benefits at much smaller expenses are sham concerns. Cornelius Walford, an insur-

---

which is about $5 annually on $1000, while in our fraternal endowment it is less than 50 cents per annum for the same amount (as we employ no agents, pay neither commissions nor salaries, except to one District Secretary); and the thinking brother can easily form his own judgment about the pretences of cheaper insurance in other societies. But facts speak louder than all arguments. The following figures are taken from the most prominent associations' own reports for 1884 to the Insurance Department:

(A). Showing the present cost per $1000 insurance in some of the oldest Assessment Societies:

The United Brethren Mutual Aid Society of Lebanon, Pa., established 1870.

Insurance in force $11,702,000—amount paid by members, $470,972; cost per $1000 = $40.27.

Ohio Mutual Relief Association. Cincinnati, O., established 1873.

Insurance in force, $1,686,000 —amount paid by members, $48,530; cost per $1000 = $23.78.

In many of the older societies the insurance in force is no definite amount

(B). Showing the ratio of expenses to losses paid in some of the leading Assessments Societies:

Mutual Reserve Fund Life Association, New York City.

Losses paid to members, $479,967 – expenses paid, $300,306. Ratio of expenses to claims paid, 62.5 per cent.

ance scholar of world-wide reputation, replied
to the question: whether he considered it an
impossibility for an assessment society to succeed? "No, I certainly do not, *provided* the
fundamental principles governing life insurance
be fully and properly recognized; but these very
principles seem to be entirely disregarded by
the assessment societies working on t..is con-
tinent."

The testimony of impartial experts, the advice
of our most devoted fellow-members, facts and
figures, experience and common sense—all combine to disabuse our brethren of these delusions;
and truth will finally conquer.

(2). DISTRUSTS, a fear of dishonesty and mis-
management—by the centralization of a large
fund and by placing it in the hands of one
Board of Trustees—has also been shown in its

Fidelity Mu ual Life Association, Philadelphia, Pa.
Losses paid to members, $51 129—expenses paid $51,910. Ratio of
expenses to claims paid, 101.5 per cent.

North-Western Masonic Aid Association, Chicago, Ill.
Losses paid to members, $468,997—expenses paid, $99,728. Ratio of
expenses to claims paid, ¬1.3 per cent.

W. & O. Endowment Fund, District Grand Lodge, No. 1,
I.O.B.B., New York.
Losses paid to members, $100 000—expenses paid, $2066. Ratio of
expenses to claims paid, 2.0 per cent. *Sapiente Sat.*

futility. The history of District No. 5 has illustrated the great evils of charging the lodges with the custody and management of fractional parts of the endowment fund ; while NO District that has placed its fund in the care of one Board of Trustees has sustained any loss what-ever. Moreover, it should be remembered that the reserve fund being from time to time in-vested, as it accumulates, in bonds and mort-gages, there are never more than a few thousand dollars in cash money on hand, for which the treasurer gives ample security. True, we often hear of defalcations ; but it is no less true that innumerable more trusts are honestly discharged. The hundreds of millions held in trust and annually paid out by our monetary institutions to rightful owners and beneficiaries, provide the truest evidence this argument may require ; and only the vilest carper will hint that WE have no honest, trustworthy men.

(3). PREJUDICES. There prevail, among some of the best and brightest of our members, pre-conceived opinions of a more respectable char-acter—notions which, though incorrect, still seem to be none the less firmly rooted. The men possessed of these notions think the endowment to be, after all, nothing different from ordinary life insurance ; they believe that it should be *optional ;* that it is selfish, not germane to the objects of the Order--NOT A CHARITY.

The wonderful growth of life insurance, especially in this country₅--notwithstanding the failures of many mismanaged companies, and the distrust cast thereby on all similar associations--present the most eloquent testimony and

---

5. Policies in force at end of 1884, in twenty nine regular Life Insurance Companies, reporting to the Insurance Department of the State of New York, amounted to $1,870,728,059.00 in 750,567 policies. *Ten* of these companies hold assets amounting to over two hundred and sixty million dollars ! There are a number of smaller insurance companies, doing a local business only, and not reporting to the New York Insurance Department. Then there are, besides, the numerous assessment, or so-called co-operative insurance societies and fraternal organizations, wherein over a million people have placed their dependence for the future protection of their widows and orphans. The aggregate amount of life insurance now in force in the United States of America is fully FIVE THOUSAND MILLION DOLLARS.

View this as we may—it proves one thing beyond all doubt: that millions of people recognize life insurance as a necessity.

the best proof that "human science has never devised a more admirable plan for securing at the same time the benefit of association and the independence of the individual." There may yet be and, no doubt, still are some objectionable features in the systems, some defects in the methods of the life insurance business ; but FRATERNAL INSURANCE, divested of all speculative features, of all opportunities for profit or dividends, either to the insured, while living, or to the managers; simply providing a certain protection and assistance to every brother's widow and orphans—this cannot be considered a mere business. Life insurance is recognized as a moral and social duty for every man of family, and especially for the man of small means. What right has a man to become the head of a family, knowing it would be in utter want the moment he dies ? Only the man void of all noble, generous feelings, caring for nobody else—not even for his wife and children, only he can refuse to deny himself *five cents a day*, to forego, perhaps, one glass of beer or a cigar—in order to secure to them the endowment of one thousand dollars, that may protect them from want in the event of his death. There is a class

of selfish men, who say : " Let the women and
children earn their living as we did." These
are men with whom duty is nothing, greed
everything; but such men, if such exist among
Israelites, cannot be B'nai B'rith. Furthermore,
to protect the widows and orphans of our departed brethren is one of the principles and
objects of the Order, and would be no less a
duty towards the widow and orphans of a brother
who might not have contributed—were it optional—as towards those brethren who had
taxed themselves to provide an endowment.
Would not this be unjust ?   Would we not
thereby rob the unselfish brother for the benefit of
the selfish one? Then it certainly is proper and
germane to the objects of the Order that every
member be required to contribute to the Widow
and Orphan Endowment Fund. And he should
do so for his own sake as well, as it tends to
preserve self-respect and freedom from anxiety.
Let the wealthy brother, whose family is amply
provided for (and such are but few), bequeath
his endowment to his lodge for the benefit of its
poorer members (as some have already done).

" O, what a precious comfort 'tis to have so many,
Like brothers, commanding one another's fortunes."
                              —*Timon of Athens*.

Some eminent, but too idealistic and not very practical, members of the Order believe to stigmatize the *endowment* by saying: "It is no charity." True, it is no charity "that renders good for evil, blessings for curses;" it is something far superior: IT MAKES CHARITY UNNECESSARY; it does "on mutual wants build mutual happiness." Which one of us would ever wish his wife and children to depend on charity? In days of old our fathers prayed at the conclusion of each meal that ours may never eat the bread of charity. We, as B'nai B'rith, offer the same prayer in our way; to do good, to work and watch for ourselves and our fellowmen, is our form of prayer.

Therefore, let us not be misled by glittering phrases concerning *higher* objects of our Order. There are but few higher objects than that of providing mutually for our widows and orphans.

"He gives but little who gives his tears;
He gives his best who aids and cheers;
He does well, in the forest wild,
Who slays the monster and saves the child;
But he does best, and he merits more,
Who keeps the wolf from the widow's door!"

Let us do this honestly, wisely; and, "*sustained and soothed by an unfaltering trust, approach our End.*"

CONTENTS.

PART I.—EARLY HISTORY.

PART II.—1874–1879.

274

www.ingramcontent.com/pod-product-compliance
Lightning Source LLC
Chambersburg PA
CBHW021058030726
47496CB00006B/1889